NOWHITHER: THE DROWNED WORLD

BOOK TWO OF THE UNWITHERING REALM

JOHN C. WRIGHT

Ebook ISBN 978-1-925645-89-7

Print ISBN 978-1-925645-90-3

"The men of the East may spell the stars,
And times and triumphs mark,
But the men signed of the cross of Christ
Go gaily in the dark."
— **G.K. Chesterton**

PROLOGUE: WHERE WAS I?

*T*hey had kidnapped the girl I had a crush on, so I was going to knock down their damned tower and destroy their planet.

Yes, I admit that I've never *actually* destroyed a planet before, and I had no means to do it. Or even a hint that this was possible. On the other hand, the goal was simple and straightforward: Kill the Bad Guys. What I did not have was the means or opportunity. But, oh, I had the motive. I was driven.

Why so mad? First, because of the girl. Second, they had already opened a beachhead in an interdimensional war with Earth and killed twice as many people in one hour than died in the whole Second World War. Third...

Third, my mother was not dead, despite the funeral Dad held for her after she vanished. She was alive and stranded on a world half-poisoned by the twilight effect of the Dark Tower, trapped and unable to get back to me.

Here is the setup: there are many earths, just like they teach you in Physics class. But not every event creates a split, only miraculous events.

In our world, for example, the human race spread out from North Africa to all continents, forming different races, tribes and nations, each with a different language. In the world of the Dark Tower, there was one race, one tribe, and one language, and by knowing this original first language of man, they understood all languages. They did not understand the idea that people could or should be independent.

Astrology, which in our world is a joke, in their world actually works. The Lords of the Darkest Tower can predict the future, and I mean in such exact detail that, first, they win every war, even if they know which battles they will lose while doing it, and, second, they go insane, because they know exactly what is happening in their lives ahead of time, who they are going to marry and when they are going to die. Everything. The prison they had me in was nothing compared to that.

When they discovered the Moebius gate, and found ways to travel across the Twilight between worlds, the Dark Tower vowed to conquer all. Not just conquering Europe, like Napoleon, not just the World, like the Nazis. Everything.

Turns out that the Vatican has secretly known about the worlds beyond the Moebius gate since the Middle Ages, and kept it secret. The Knights Templar, which history says were destroyed on our world, are still in business elsewhere, and are fighting back against the Dark Tower.

My Dad, who is not my dad at all, is one of them. Turns out my older brothers, Alexei and Dobrin are Templars also. They are tall and blond. I look like a Neanderthal with buck teeth. They are not really my brothers.

My name is Ilya Muromets. Yes, I was named after a great hero from legend. And yes, I have always wanted to live up to that name.

No, my last name is not Marmoset. It is an understandable mistake when a girl I have a crush on makes it. Anyone else, I would punch in the face. No mocking the name.

My best friend is Foster Hidden. He is a gypsy, and he is dark and suave and handsome. We were in Boy Scouts together. But he is not what he seems either. Foster is a spy from some elf-haunted world from a German opera, and he knows the secret of how to cloud men's minds, like the Invisible Girl or something.

Turns out, he is an agent of a group called the Wisecraft, who are witches and wizards from various worlds also opposing the Dark Tower. His real name is Eflast Falinn the Ringbearer. Yes, he has got a magic arm-ring that turns him invisible.

And my girl, who is not my girl, because she hardly knows I exist, is not named Penelope Dreadful after all, but Parthenope. She is a mermaid, except she has legs. Shapely legs. I am not sure what that makes her. A siren? A Rhine-maiden? A waterbender?

Her mission was to rescue a stern old man named Ossifrage out of the Dark Tower. He is some sort of prophet or something. At least, he looks like Charlton Heston playing Moses. His real name, you do not want to know. He is a cloud-walker, a master of levitation.

As for the headless giant who was going to eat me, but who changed his mind when I rescued him out of jail, his name is Nakasu. He is a creature called a Blemmye, and he keeps his face in his chest. Call him Knack.

I had been rescued out of jail in turn by a little girl in a monkey-mask, somewhere between twelve and fourteen, who could blind the predictions of the astrologers. They could not foretell her actions because of some sort of magic water she bathed in. I was not too clear on the details.

Her name was She-Monkey, Pagutu, but her higher and secret name she told me was Abanshaddi, the Mountain

Rock, so I called her Abby. She and I are blood-brother and blood-sister. I had to adopt her. You do not want to know what they did to her mother. But that was yet another reason to hate the Dark Tower, and the damned astrologers.

Me? I am immortal. I cannot die. Stab me, I just get better.

Don't think of this as some sort of mutant healing factor or regeneration. Think of this as freaking nuts, as in I can do thinks like cut off my own head and carry it around in my hand like the horseman from Legend of Sleepy Hollow.

You would think that would make things easy on me, seeing as I cannot be killed.

I wish.

So that was the group. We also had with us over a hundred slavegirls from the harem where Penny had been imprisoned. I was not going to leave them behind.

We also had a portable Moebius coil that unfolded from the royal flail the ghost of a Pharaoh had given me. Thanks to Nakasu, who got the thing to turn on, thanks to Ossifrage, who capsized the ironclad airship attacking us, thanks to Abby, who messed up the Astrologer's predictions, and thanks to Foster, who hid us with his mists of invisibility, we all fell through the black orb of the dimensional gateway.

And we got away.

We escaped from the Dark Tower from which no one ever escapes. We should not have, but, somehow, we did.

And the damsel I was here to rescue had actually, officially been rescued. This meant, despite everything else that had gone wrong or grossed me out, I was actually, officially, a hero. Which is basically what I have wanted to be since I was a kid.

So now I could die happy. Except I could not die.

We were still in deadly danger every moment, but it was still a good day for me.

ASSAULT IN THE ATRIUM

1. ENTER STAGE RIGHT

If they ever make a movie version of my life, the transition through the Moebius coil from the aeon of Ur to the next aeon would be dignified yet impressive, with special effects showing dark winds swirling about my newly-elongated hair, and the actor representing me will stand, maybe with a torn shirt to show off his sun-brazen yet manly chest, legs spread, head high, every inch the hero who just saved over a hundred slaves and victims of the cruelty of the Dark Tower. He will shimmer into existence like Captain Kirk, surrounded by soaring chords of some famous movie theme by Eric Wolfgang Korngold. It will be great.

Of course, if they ever do make that movie, I will have to bribe or threaten Foster to keep his big mouth shut. What actually happened is that I popped out of a dark sphere on the far side upside down, tangled in the huge yards of hair I had accidentally popped out of my skull, and I made a noise like a yodeler at a yodeling contest who was disqualified on account of a squeak in the middle of his bawl.

And I landed on my face.

The surface I landed on was a black mirror, like a floor of dark silver, in a room as large as a gymnasium. Black square pillars stood to each side along with large square doors like truck bays. The room was lit by thin arrow slits high in the ceiling. The walls were inscribed with a row of astrological zodiacs, king-faced bulls, centaurs, and cuneiform writing. Foster was nearby, doubled over, laughing at me.

Important safety tip: aways sheathe your grandfather's katana before doing a summersault from one dimension to the next. Thanks to my chainmail, I was not cut badly, and thanks to my mutant regeneration power, I was able to press the cut shut and pray it into sealing. I won't mention where I cut myself; it was an embarrassing spot, one that would make the guys in the emergency room giggle if I had been a normal mortal.

But I wasn't. I was a Toon; as indestructible as Yosemite Sam blown to smithereens by a Bronx rabbit armed with a box of dynamite. So no wonder Foster laughed.

2. BETWEEN WORLDS PARENTHETICAL

Let me hit the pause button for a second and tell you in excruciating detail what it looked like when I passed through the Moebius coil because it was weird, and I cannot quite figure out what I was looking at. Pay attention because there may be a quiz later.

From the point of view of someone passing through a Moebius coil, the surface is a black sphere before you reach it. That is the Deep you are looking at.

When you pass through the surface, the blackness seems to swell into a convex surface, then a flat wall you are about to smash into, then a concave surface, and then a sphere again that is like a bubble of air, this time with you inside it. You are in one hemisphere falling toward the middle. The inner surface of the bubble of air shows a distorted picture of the world you are leaving. Now imagine that you shrink down to the size of a dot as you near the center of the sphere, or, rather, that the image of the world painted on the inside of an elastic balloon expands and turns darker.

At the center of the sphere, when you pass through the parallel rings of the coil, the image seems to open up into a roaring tunnel for just a second, and it looks exactly the way an interdimensional gateway should look: like a rushing black-gray-azure tube of nothingness.

The next instant, you are englobed in a fish-eye image of the world you are entering, as if the scene is painted on the inside of a balloon that is collapsing rapidly. As you fall away from the center, in front of you the picture gets undistorted, going from a concave surface to flat and normal space. Behind you, if you look—and I did because we were being chased—the darkness does the same inside-out flip in reverse, going from a tunnel to a concavity to a flat wall and shrinking to the sphere surface you are leaving. Then, you pop out. From the outside, the ball is all dark.

And there is no gravity in the middle, so it feels just like being in an elevator when the cable snaps or on a fairground ride that makes you want to upchuck.

So picture it this way: the left hemisphere of the globe, when you are inside it, shows the departure world all around you rushing away; the right hemisphere shows the destination world rushing inward; in between, the long moment when you pass through the focus at the center of the globe, it does not look like a globe at all but like falling down a well.

The equator of the bubble consists of the parallel twin rings of the transmitting and receiving Moebius coils, and

7

from our point of view they look like they are pressed up against each other as tightly as possible. I assume the receiver and the transmitter rings have to be placed in the exact same spot in Uncreation space.

The seal is not perfect: there is a whistling shriek like a teakettle as atmosphere escapes under the pressure of fifteen pounds per square inch from reality into unreality.

I wondered if centuries of using the Moebius coil technology had diminished the atmosphere on the aeon of Ur by any appreciable extent. Of course, they could always pipe in air from worlds they conquered if it ever became a measurable problem.

I also assume that the first time I fell through, and ended up in the Uncreation itself, happened because some technician was still making adjustments to the Vernier dials while trying to get a fix on the aperture to Earth. I had fallen through before the docking maneuver, or whatever it was called, was ready.

This time the rings were lined up and docked, so I did not actually hit the Oobleck. During the moment when I passed down the tube, I saw and felt the dark stuff of Uncreation whirl past me, and I felt a strange sense of strength enter my limbs.

Do you remember that weirdbeard feeling I got when Rahab came close? Something like that happened when I passed through. I could not shake the weird feeling that someone or something out there in the darkness was thinking about me and was watching me during that momentary transition between world and world.

Freaky.

3. DANGEROUS PEOPLE

I scrambled to my feet and spun. Behind me were three Moebius coils standing upright on the dais where I stood. Call them Papa Bear, Mama Bear, and Baby Bear. The golden circle of the pharaoh's flail—call it our portable hole—had been lying prone. Which explains my clumsiness in entering: the gravity had been perpendicular to the gate I swan-dived into and parallel to the gate I pratfalled out of.

Papa Bear was the size of a railroad tunnel mouth, and Mama Bear was wider than a barn door. Baby Bear, about eight feet across, was the one we had come through.

It was still active: in the center of the ring was a whirling globe of darkness surrounded by an aurora borealis.

I shouted, "Someone shut the gate! They are right behind me!" But I kept my eyes on the fiery black sphere, and both hands on my katana, and so did not look around.

No one answered. A noise like an earthquake jarred my back teeth.

I risked a quick look over my shoulder.

That noise was just Nakasu toppling one of the huge square pillars with his monstrous strength. The ceiling creaked—never a good sign—and Ossifrage wafted the Volkswagen-sized blocks of stone over in front of a portcullis larger than a garage door.

Nakasu must have knocked quite a few pillars over because there were three other piles of rubble blocking the sally ports. I could smell the acrid, metal shop smell of burning metal and could see door was beginning to turn cherry red.

It is never a good sign when you are trapped in a strange room in a strange fortress on an unknown world and the guys on the other side of a door have something that is melting it.

And that is not all; the *boom, boom* of a battering ram echoed through the chamber, and the cherry red spot on the portcullis was beginning to bow outward. Then, Ossifrage piled more square boulders atop the portcullis, and it was lost to sight momentarily.

I looked around.

The chamber was octagonal, larger than a railway roundhouse, with a number of Moebius coils of various sizes set upright near the walls. Each coil stood atop a dais made of wood.

Some coils were as big as train tunnels and straight or curved black roadways of living metal linked one dais to another so that a Wayship zooming out one coil could pass to the next without slowing. Each black roadway looked like an ebony lawn of iron grass. It implied that not all coils could be tuned to each other because, otherwise, why have more than two coils in a station?

Against the wall were several garage doors to which sidetracks ran. One door was up; triangular crates of a size that would fit neatly into a Wayship were stacked in a vast warehouse beyond like cordwood.

One wall was dominated by a portcullis flanked by sally ports and hemicylinders that looked like bartizans. This was where the rubble was piled, where the muffled booming of the battering ram rang. The hinges were on our side, which meant the gates were built to keep those inside the chamber locked in, not to keep outsiders locked out.

Along the walls opposite the gate was a bank of clockwork calculation engines tall enough that it took two levels of ladders to reach the top. Above this hung a noticeboard written over in cuneiform. Tanks or cisterns stood against other walls, cranes, and derricks. And everywhere were statues of winged bulls and little grinning gnomes with goggle eyes.

In the zenith of the dome was a thing like an inverted cupola, a little balcony or deck. It was armored like a pillbox with catapults like huge crossbows pointed downward across the balcony rail in each direction.

There were also a group of three or four fresh corpses with broken bones lying in a pool of blood right below it, as if Ossifrage had levitated them out and across the balcony and dropped them. There was a mass of six or seven more corpses littered here and there around the room; one of them looked like an immense force had spun him by one leg head-first into the wall so that his brain stuff and blood sprayed in a bright red triangle of dripping mess like a burst water-balloon.

Ossifrage and Nakasu had killed all the guards and ware-housemen in the few seconds I had taken talking with Enmeduranki.

"We're dangerous people," I muttered. "If I weren't us, I'd be afraid of us."

All the cute teen girls were huddled near the center of the chamber, big eyed and quaking like a doe that scents a hunter. The girl who was a snake from the waist down and a Bollywood actress from the waist up had made a protective semicircle with her sea-serpent tail around a group of them, a protective but pathetic gesture. There were too many for anyone to shield.

Think of a cafeteria or assembly in an all-girls school or college. That was how many lives I was responsible for. A bunch of girls whose names I did not even know.

4. TRAPPED

Abby said, "We have taken them unaware."

I said, "Little Sister, this is them with their pants down?"

She is not really my little sister, but I felt she needed an older brother to beat up whoever picked on her, and I nominated myself to the post. Come to think of it, she was no less my family than anyone else in my family, if you take my meaning.

Abby said, "They wear kirtles. But, yes. If they had been prepared, they could have simply poured boiling oil and hot tar through those spouts in the ceiling on us. Oil takes time to heat."

Foster had sunk down to one knee and was leaning on his bowstaff. Ossifrage was throwing more rubble on the doors as fast as Nakasu could Sampson the pillars down. The graduating class of ex-slavegirls was cowering and huddling. I did not blame them: but I suppose the ones who were brave and defiant had been weeded out during their first week of captivity, long ago. Penny was standing near the piles of rubble, singing.

And Abby was looking at me expectantly. As if I were the one who was going to come up with the great idea. As if someone had died and left me the boss.

I didn't get it. Nakasu was a grown adult, and Ossifrage was grown and white-haired; Foster was a dark elf gypsy secret agent who was in the know, and Penny was a mermaid even more in the know. Abby was a child, but she was familiar with the Dark Tower and all its works and all its ways.

What was it about me that made people care about my opinion? It sure wasn't my looks. And my new hairdo was not going to win any awards.

There were no windows here, except the arrow slits, and no doors. No way out.

Abby said, "It will not take the garrison long to gather men against us."

I heard horns blowing and bells ringing in the distance.

5. MURDER HOLES

Wild Eyes was sitting on Penny's wrist and now puffed up her feathers and made a noise as frantic as a steam whistle. "Darts!" The little creature shrieked in English. Abby called out, "Arrows!" for the benefit the non-English speakers.

Ossifrage stepped up into midair so that he was above the shrieking crowd of girls and waved his shepherd crook overhead. A dozen or two dozen arrows shot into the chamber from hidden loops or murder holes set in the wall above the portcullis. The flight of arrows parted like the Red Sea for Charlton Heston, impaled themselves into crates or equipment or fresh corpses placed here and there about the chamber, or clattered from the mirrored floor or the metal tracks.

Foster shot an arrow straight and true into the wall and through the tiny arrow loop. The slit was maybe nine inches wide, and he was maybe sixty feet away and shooting upward at an awkward angle. It was a bullseye. I heard a man's hoarse scream from beyond the wall. Confusion and commotion as pale mist staring pouring out, first from that arrow slit and from all the others to the left and right. My eyes crossed and refused to focus, and I could not see the mist or the arrow slits. I assume the whole squad of archers on the balcony behind the murder holes was blinded for the moment.

This was a pretty big amount of inviso power Foster had raised pretty quickly, and, from the look of the strain on his face, Foster was not likely to be able to keep it up for long. I could see little sweat tears of blue woad beginning to trickle down his forehead.

I wanted to talk to Penny, but she was across the chamber from me, singing an odd, haunting song that throbbed with the throbbing of my heart, and I could hear in my ears a sound like the sound trapped in a seashell. My heartbeat felt like the tide, ebbing and flowing, and I was swaying on my feet in a moment.

She was not even singing her song at me. What I caught was just the backscatter. But the sound of the battering ram hesitated, thumped one last weak thump, and halted. I suppose I only imagined the sound of snores from beyond the melting portcullis beneath the rubble.

But her face was as pink as Foster's was blue. She had already given several opera-voice- -reaching-the-back-row performances in the last hour of so. She was too busy to talk to, and, unless we both took a crash course on American Sign Language in the next moment, her voice was completely occupied.

Foster was panting from exertion, but he spoke just as calmly as Abby, "By the way, we're trapped."

I said to him, "You don't seem upset."

He said, "Since lunchtime, I have talked a cranky hawk into releasing me from a cage made of electrified barbed wire, ran buck naked through the hall of the Dark Tower without getting caught, fought a witch of Illyria and her wolfmen in a museum, recovered all my gear *and* my crazy pal Ilya, was flung through the upper atmosphere by a cranky Old Testament prophet, raided a harem full of shapely college girls dressed in slinky underwear, pulled a vampire out of a coffin, saved a hundred people from his hypnotic death-gaze, and then faced the Lord of Magicians himself, the master of the Dark Tower, fighting the elite troopers of his mask-faced floating superdreadnought, which fired on us point blank and, thanks to me, missed, and I have been escaping certain death without any major wounds, and I got to see the feminine charms of many charming females in a charming state of semi-undress, including the voluptuous Miss Dreadful." He shrugged. "This has been a good day for me."

"I think she is within earshot, charming boy."

"And I am in shock, so I am not responsible for what I am saying. LOOK OUT!"

And he raised his bow, nocked an arrow, and shot it faster than I could have snapped my fingers. It whistled past my shoulder.

I spun. Soldiers in bronze helmets and metal jackets and skirts were emerging from the sphere. Do not think of a tunnel mouth: some came out from the left, some from the right, some from the rear hemisphere. I could not see the ones in the rear, but I could hear their brass horns braying and see the tips of their spears above the upper curve. A flying pygmy with a blowgun was rising up from the upper curve of the black ball.

I heard the voices of a hundred girls behind me screaming in fear.

6. MOEBIUS SERPENT

With a shout of alarm, I jumped toward the black sphere. The soldier right before me had a glass arrow protruding from his chest, and a mist radiated from the glass, and he vanished from my sight. The next man behind him emerging from the black sphere surface was confused, groping, blinded by the magic mist of the same glass arrow that hid his friend.

I was right at his feet, and he did not see me. I knelt and put my hand inside the sphere right at the equator where the Moebius coil bisected it. I knew the two rings were side by side even though, from this world, I could only see the upright receiving ring. I felt the painful suction like a thin line across my palm. This was the tiny air gap between the two rings. The energies released by the action of the Moebius coil heated up the gold, so I could feel my hand, even through the leather palms of my gauntlet, burn to the bone. A human would have been crippled. But I could feel under my burning fingers, just by dumb luck, one of the ruby rings that controlled the flail. I twisted the ring and opened the circle.

I am assuming that to the Great King Anshargal and Enmeduranki the Dark Lord, and to all the other guys on the inner balcony of the Dark Tower rushing toward where the portable hole was sitting on the ground, projecting a hemisphere of darkness, it must have looked like an ordinary hand reaching out at ground level and grabbing the rigid gold circle, unsnapping it and drawing it into the black surface, which instantly collapsed.

I am assuming my hand must have seemed like a gigantic and fish-eye distorted trunk of flesh reaching all the way down the tunnel to the king's men passing through the Moebius coil.

The invisible dead man fell, and the man behind him now saw me. I was too close for him to use his spear. He dropped his spear and clutched toward my throat with his free hand. I hit him with a head-butt like an angry ram, so he stumbled and started to fall back into the black sphere. He grabbed the loose fold of chain mail at my throat.

I drove the point of Dancing Maiden into the black sphere at the spot where his body was last seen. It was a blind blow, but I connected with something. I brought Dancing Maiden on the backstroke up and through his arm grabbing at me, and jumped back, with the now-limp flail in my left hand like a three-tailed golden snake, still burning and glittering with extradimensional energies. It was a well-executed stroke despite the awkward angle and being one-handed. I cleaved through radius and ulna, gushing veins and arteries and all.

Then came a noise like the end of the world. It was as if a

bomb had gone off in the atrium chamber, but one that exploded inward, not outward. An implosion.

As quickly and as far as I jumped back, I was almost far enough away when the wavefront hit me. Almost.

Remember that teakettle whistle? Well, now fifteen pounds per square inch picked me up like a leaf in a hurricane and threw me straight toward the shrinking black ball.

7. EXPLOSIVE DECOMPRESSION

Have you ever seen a sci-fi flick where some astronaut disengages the safety override and blasts open both the inner and outer airlock but somehow manages to cling to a stanchion for a moment while the nasty alien is blown into outer space?

Well, that is the scene where you might as well get up and get yourself a second tub of popcorn because you are not missing anything that could actually really happen in real life, unless the astronaut is from the planet Krypton.

Do a little back-of-the-envelope calculation on how much weight would be pushed against your astronaut and then compare it to the weight you can bench press. I'll get you started: at fifteen pounds per square inch, thirty-two square inches equals 480 pounds, which is more than I bench. The average human body has three thousand square inches of surface.

So there was no clinging to anything for me. It would have ripped my arms out of my sockets had I tried.

The soldiers, men and wolves and winged things, emerging from the sphere were yanked back into it. They could not have resisted the air pressure any more than they could have resisted an avalanche of iron boulders or a sixty-foot tidal wave.

But the sphere was shrinking, and it was only the size of

my head, and too small for my shoulders, when I rammed into it at, I dunno, call it Mach One.

Don't imagine this like a man with his head stuck in a porthole of a ship, with his shoulders bumping up against the wall to either side. It was not like that. There was a sphere of airlessness right in front of my face, and my face went into it, and one atmosphere of pressure was like a superhurricane wind blowing from every point of the sphere inward toward the nothingness ball in which my head was lodged. I could not move my head left or right, up or down, fore or back, because the pressure would force me to the center again. I could not shove my head further into the fourth dimension because the aperture was a smaller diameter than my shoulders.

My head was in the place that was between the worlds.

Everything went silent. I could see the Uncreation.

It was boiling, writhing, blending, streaming, shrinking, growing, shivering, flickering. It was a blind spot; it was madness.

Now for the quiz I promised: what happens to the squad inside the tunnel during inter-dimensional transit if someone collapses the transmitting Moebius coil from a ring shape to a limp golden snake and yanks the snake out through the receiver?

I saw what happened.

There was a line of soldiers tumbling end over end in the utter nothingness. They were dying without being allowed to utter a sound. Their shields and spears where spreading out from them, dropping, if that is the word, in an expanding globe away from the writhing agony-twisted figures.

I could *see* their fear because the silent shrieks of their dying souls, the terror of the disaster, was turning the ylem all around them into a smoky blue-black fire, reaching for them like the snakes of the hair of the Medusa, solidifying around them, strangling, constricting, burning.

By picking up the Moebius gate from this side and yanking it through, I had severed the connection between the two points in normal space. It was like cutting the supports of a rope bridge over some South American canyon, except instead of a steaming jungle river at the bottom, there was a void.

Then came a thunderclap.

The black sphere popped like a soap bubble.

However, I was looking *up* at my hand. My severed head was sitting in the area between the upright ring of the now-empty Baby Bear-sized Moebius coil and the back wall.

My headless body was on its feet, swaying, toppled forward, and fell next to me, blood gushing like a firehose from my neck stump.

8. INCONSISTENT IMPOSSIBILITIES

The whole atrium was shining with blinding blue-white light, *ylemaramu*, which was shining from the daises on which the Moebius coils stood, but only on the far side the chamber. The daises were made of lampwood, which makes sense if you think about it: it was designed to quell any residue of twilight in the chamber and to close any remaining gateways into a vacuum larger than the cosmos. Otherwise, the whole planet might lose its atmosphere.

Remember what I said about those space movies where astronauts can just resist the pressure of explosive decompression by holding onto something? Well, if you stick your head through a breech in your hull, but your shoulders are too broad to fit through, the wind shear should yank your head off. Fortunately for me, the decapitation process was slow enough that the black sphere had winked out before it was done, so my head was not lost between dimensions.

That would have been inconvenient.

I wondered if, after decapitation, my body would grow a new head from the neck stump upward, and, if so, the brain would have my personality and memories; and meanwhile my head grow a new body from the neck stump downward. If so, I could create my own clone army of me! I was in the middle of calculating where I could get a working guillotine when I mentally yanked thoughts back to noncrazyland, startled to see how even a short period of immortality warps your thinking.

From my position on the now-blue-lit floor, there seemed to be relatively little wreckage throughout the chamber. I assume me getting my head stuck in the black ball had plugged it like a sink stopper for a moment so that everyone behind me had not been yanked through.

But where was everyone? The chamber for a moment seemed empty of people.

I could not turn my head, but I rolled my eyes left and right. The dais I stood on, and all the ones to the left and right of me were not lit up, nor any dais near a broken pillar.

About that time, I realized that the high-pitched shrieking I heard was not the high-pitched shrieking of the indoor hurricane, but an all-girls' choir of one hundred and fifty screaming in panic. I was able to jerk my jaw hard enough to the left to roll my head and point my eyes upward.

Ossifrage was in the darkest reach of the dome, in the corner where the cupola dangled from the roof like a stalactite, and his power did not fail. Ossifrage was holding the gaggle of girls in the chamber in midair, so none had been dashed against the floor or the walls by the catastrophe. Ossifrage was holding Penny and Foster, both of them upside down as if caught in midfall while being flung from a bucking bronco, so, unfortunately, his mist spell and her lullaby had been interrupted.

Penny had very nice legs, which were displayed to their best advantage with her short skirts falling up rather than down. Foster was staring at her despite his awkward angle. I decided he had no class at all. What a cur. Me? My excuse is that I could not turn my head.

Fortunately, there was also considerable shrieking coming from beyond the wall pierced by murder holes, shouting, commotion, trumpets, alarums, and excursions. The sound was falling off rapidly. It was the sound of a company of men in full retreat. Retreat? No, a rout. They were fleeing pell-mell.

Nakasu was on the side of the chamber where the *ylemaramu* was burning bright and was not levitating. He was holding on to a metal clamp affixed to the wall with both hands and his enormous belly-teeth: I revised my estimate of his strength upward. And he had a lot more surface area than a human being, so more pressure had been on him. This was a feat of strength equivalent to bench pressing more than six times his body weight. Maybe he was from Krypton.

Wild Eyes landed right next to me and looked at my left eye hungrily. In her angry steam-whistle shrill, she shouted, "Foolish boy! Idiotic! Reckless! Would you kill us all!" She drew back her beak to hammer the point into my precious eyeball jelly.

But I could still feel my body. The same way I sensed where my severed hand had been after the fight in the Chamber of Rarities, I was still in control of my headless, neck-fountaining lump of me-meat. It was like trying to move your character in a shooter game were you are not familiar with the controller, so I could not exactly parry the incoming beak with my normal way-cool samurai sword-dude skills. Instead, my body awkwardly toppled forward like a felled pine, the bird squawked and hopped out of the way, glaring, and I ended up with my own armpit cradling my poor, battered skull, but with eyeballs safely out of beak-range.

Unsteadily, I rose to my feet, cradling my head in my wobbly hands at belt buckle level. I tried to moan, "Ichabod Crane! I am coming for you!" but my severed head had no lungs to push the words out.

That seemed really unfair to me. I mean, I could do impossible things, like slurp all my spilled blood backward through midair and into the veins and arteries in my neck (dull red into the arteries, bright red into the veins), but I could not talk without lungs? Some impossible things I could do without blinking, but then when I tried something else, the laws of nature suddenly woke up like a snoozing beat cop in a donut shop and enforced the letter of the law? Ridiculous!

2

THE WITHERED WORLD

1. RECAPITATION

*T*he noise from beyond the wall fell to nothing. The defenders had pulled back.

Penny dropped down from the sky and stepped over. Even though I had no lungs, my nose was still working, and I could smell her girl-under-exertion smell (you can call it sweat if you like, but on her it smelled good—*real* good), and, shooing back her bird with a frown, worried my head out from under my arm, and pushed it up to my neck hole.

"Good work, hero," she said in a dry, sardonic tone. Her voice was slightly husky from the singing she'd been doing lately. "Plugging the hole between dimensions with your head was a stroke of genius. It saved us from being yanked into the Deep. But next time warn us."

Now you would think if there was no connection running from my testosterone-producing groin glands to my head, I would be as pure in thought as a monk. Unless that monk is Rasputin, my thoughts were nothing like that.

My head was slipping out of my remote-controlled hands.

As she plucked me out of my own nerveless grasp, I could feel her soft hands and long fingers cradling my cheeks, her palms over my ears. As she picked up my head, and my eyes were nine inches from her narrow, silk-covered waist. The magnificent swell of her bosom passed before my eyes even closer. I next saw the delicate line of her collarbone and neck, and then I was being held over her head, and she was trying to hold my two neck halves together. She was standing on tiptoe, which is such a cute posture that the entire shoe industry, or perhaps the Spanish Inquisition, had invented the high heel just to make women assume that position as often as possible. My nose was near her nose, and her head was back, and her lips slightly parted, and her hands on my cheeks holding tight, which, while being the position a girl must assume to prop your head back on your neck, is also kissing posture. But she straightened her arms, and the lips grew farther away.

By the time I had my head screwed on straight—and I won't describe the grisly spaghetti sensation of all my vertebrae and windpipes and blood vessels seeking their mates—the moment for Sleepy Hollow jokes had passed. Some of the girls were bleeding. Most were crying softly.

Ossifrage had lowered the girls to the ground and was bent over, wheezing, wearily waving his crook as if to keep the stray arrows from hitting him: but no arrows were flying. I could not see if he was wounded or just winded. Foster's mist was still stuffed into the archer's slits. I could tell because I could not see the murder holes. Foster had been dropped supine and was on the ground, panting. I did not see any arrows in him.

When I got my throat tubes reconnected, I said to Abby, "Little Sister, what's going on? What happened to the attack?"

Abby said back, "They are donning their *Nahlapt-Aqara-pas-bet*." Armor for when air is gaspingly thin. Pressure suits.

I looked at the dome. "Is there any other way out of here? A small door or hatch? Someplace in that copula overhead?"

"Don't these people believe in fire exits?" groaned Foster from where he slumped.

Penny said, "None of them step into rooms where the astrologers foresee there will be a fire. There are no accidents in the Ur world."

I decided no sane man could ever get used to their freakish world.

Abby, meanwhile, had repeated my question to Ossifrage and Nakasu. Ossifrage said something in Hebrew, and I caught the gist: *If I knew another way out, don't you think we'd be there now?* Nakasu's comment was in Swahili, and Abby translated it as, "This is a major station house. The walls are made airtight so that if a Coilpath is severed, as you did just now, only one room becomes airless."

I realized that I was not seeing the murder holes not because they were misted over but because they were clamped shut. The chamber was hermetically sealed.

Nakasu pointed at the damaged pillars and spoke again. Abby translated. "I disconnected the safety lamps so that the Station Master could not flood the chamber with starbloodlight and close the Coilpath before you crossed over."

I said to Abby, "What is starbloodlight? Is it the same thing as *ylemaramu*?"

She nodded, "Such is the word in the tongue of Sabtah."

I wondered why his people would pick such a word for a blue eye-dazzling light, but this was not time for philological curiosity. I said, "We have to Moebius out of here. Nakasu! Can you work these station controls? Open a gate?"

I tossed him the now-flexible golden lengths of the flail. When he caught it, the haft straightened up with a metallic chime of noise. I pointed at the three upright Moebius coils next to me.

Nakasu, with a grin on his belly and a squint on his pectorals, now stepped forward, but not toward the coils. He moved to the two-story-tall clockwork machine of brass gears and pistons, jumping up to the catwalk without bothering with the ladder, and craning back his shoulders to study the cuneiform characters of the board overhead.

When he cranked certain wheels, hands on what looked like seven-handed clocks clicked forward and back through twelve positions. Each hand was tipped with the same traditional astrological sign used on my world for the sun and moon and inner planets, plus Mars, Jupiter, and Saturn. Whenever he pulled a lever like the handle of a slot machine, the board above would clatter, and the cuneiform letters of cunning metal would click into new configurations, looking like a swarm of twitching arrowheads.

2. DISARMAMENT

I said to Abby, "Can you help me take off this haunted armor?"

The buckles ran up my spine, and I did not know Rahab's trick of elongating my arms or twisting my head on my neck like an owl.

Abby waved her hand at me, and all the coppery buckles suddenly relaxed, and the forty pounds of metal hung limp and loose like a snake's shed skin on me.

"Can everyone in Ur use their remote control hoodoo on this cunning metal stuff?"

I was sorry to part with the only thing, so far, that had saved me from all the painful, sharp, hard, and pointy things life seemed determined to stick into my undying flesh. But any enemy could turn this jerkin into a straightjacket with a thought.

Abby said calmly, "Those of the One can command the Divided."

"Then how do you fight each other? Throw away your armor and weapons?"

She looked at me oddly. "Ur do not fight Ur. The One are one."

With great reluctance, I shucked off the copper-colored cunning metal hauberk and threw it clattering to the floor. As I did so, something that looked like a brown, five-legged tarantula twitched near my foot.

It was a severed hand. Its fingers were tapping out a shaky tattoo as the nerve impulses died in it. I don't know if that is something that sometimes happens in normal worlds or not, but it scared me. I thought the hand might belong to another Undying.

Then, it died, and my fear turned glum. It was the hand that had grabbed me, which I had dismembered from its owner.

There was a ring on one finger. Was it a wedding ring, a class ring, or a present for bravery from some lord or astrologer? Did he have a wife, a family, hobbies? Did he have a paperback book he was in the middle of reading which would sit on the trunk next to his bunk back in his quarters, never to be opened again?

I tried my best not to feel sorry for the man I'd killed. I looked at all the young girls in the room and reminded myself that some folks, who might be perfectly normal guys you would not mind going with on a hunting trip, or emptying a six pack at a tailgate party before the big game, once they start working for Dark Lords and conquering and enslaving and raping and looting, were no longer just perfectly normal guys.

I had not been the one looking for this fight.

3. DESTINATION

Ossifrage led the one hundred fifty girls through the open garage door to loot the crates for anything useful, especially bandages. Ossifrage would have made the perfect warehouse manager since he could lower crates from high shelves without using a forklift or handtruck. I saw him laying hands on a girl struck with an arrow, and the arrow fell out, but whether he was just praying over the wound or whether he had healing magic, I was too ashamed to walk over close enough to see.

Yes, ashamed. Part of me said the wounds were my fault. Part of me said it wasn't my fault at all, but that part is the same part that made up excuses why I should not make my bed in the morning or wear clean underwear every day, okay?

Penny was watching Nakasu work, but her lovely eyes were narrowed as if in anger or worry.

"What's wrong?" I said to her. "We just jumped out of the jaws of the Great King's Harem. You're just sad about that date you owe me."

"You're a little too young for me, Mr. Marmoset," she said absentmindedly. "And we are not out of the belly of the beast as yet: our jump carried us no farther than from one stomach compartment to another. There is no place Nakasu can find that will not be defended. What does he mean to do?"

"I am old enough to kill your enemies," I said. "Not that I am keeping track, but there were fourteen men roped together I threw into the abyss just now, at least two dozen that got thrown from the airship into the cistern, one guy I stabbed, and one of the Host who Yearns for Death in Vain whose yearning I satisfied. That is an even forty, and that is just in the last quarter hour."

Foster, from his position sitting on the floor, called out, "He killed a witch before that. I got a room full of cynocephali, and there were forty-five of them, so I am ahead. Pointwise, I mean. Forty-five to forty-one."

Penny called out to Abby, who was in the warehouse space with Ossifrage, "Foreverborn! Ask the Blemmyae what he is doing! The Aeon of Cush is our destination."

Abby repeated the question. Nakasu answered without turning in a series of hooting snorts from his neck-blowhole. Abby said, "The Freedman says he seeks an aeon suited to himself and has little care for the goals of slaves, former slaves, future slaves, and wisecraft-workers. Pardon me, mistress, but those are his words."

I said, "Wise what?"

Foster, from the floor, said, "Wisecraft. Us."

I said to him, "I thought your people were called Knock-kneed-drunken-nutty Butter-shaft or something like that."

Foster said, "Nachtdunkelnebelritterbruderschaft. Night-Riders. That is only the cavalry arm of the Wise."

Penny snapped, "The whole alliance opposing the Dark Tower is called the Wisecraft, whose goals we all must serve if we are to survive. Mister Muromets, the Blemmyae is your responsibility. Get him to see reason!"

A sensation of cold came over me, like someone behind me had just opened the door of a walk-in meat locker. It stopped when I put my hand on the crucifix dangling from the long chain of beads I was wearing at the moment wrapped around my waist.

I looked up at the message board, all written in cuneiform, an alphabet of swarming arrowheads. "Abby! Ask Knack what world this is! The one we are on now?"

Abby did not bother asking him. She pointed at some

astrological symbols written around the base of the dome overhead and said, "This is Javan, the Withered World."

"The withered what?"

"It is the accursed land. It is ruled by the Sons of Alexander the Great, from the great capital of Pergamos, whose altars never cease to smoke."

Ossifrage uttered something in a gruff voice and spat.

Abby translated. "Bah! I know this world! For a season I was trapped here. Here, the Chosen turned their backs on the Lord of Hosts and whored after other gods. The heavenly horseman of Maccabeus never trampled Heliodorus, nor did the Maccabees prevail. The Temple was never cleansed by the oil that never failed."

Frustrating. For once I regretting not studying the Bible as closely as my brother Alexei. He would have recognized these references. Me, I could not even remember if Maccabees was an official part of the Bible or not.

Ossifrage spoke again. "It is a world of dying light, and the Abomination of Desolation erected by the Sons of Helen in the Temple of Solomon pollutes the world. It is from there the Bloodquaffers of Lilim receive their power."

Because it was Abby translating, I knew "Sons of Helen" meant Greeks. And I knew who the Bloodquaffers were.

If you have never had your head accidentally slammed in a washing machine door by your older brother, then you don't know what the sensation of having every brain cell all at once explode with the realization that you are a total idiot feels like.

This was one place it would have been perfectly safe to drop off Vorvolac.

The reason why the whole floor was plated with one huge vampire detector was that this was Vampire Grand Central, and the Dark Tower didn't want the hungry ones near the gates leading to loyal worlds filled, from the Bloodquaffer's point of view, with yummy mutton and veal.

Vorvolac was not too dangerous to live. We could have stuck him in a warehouse crate here. I could have kept my word. I could have acted like a grown-up instead of like a spooked kid.

Through gritted teeth, I said, "Little Sister, tell Knack to hurry. Any place is better than here. Even back where we were."

Penny said, "Cush is our goal!"

I snapped, "Our goal is the fabulous fun-filled land of Anydamnwhere But Here. The Bloodquaffers are coming. Look!"

Frost was beginning to form on the surface of the mirrored panels of the floor, and my breath was starting to steam.

Nakasu shouted something to Abby with his belly mouth. She said, "Everyone into the warehouse and seal the door! The abomination to yonder coil, with the sea-daughter. There is but one unwatched Coilpath of all the paths of the Dark Tower, and I have found it!"

I ran to where he pointed, one of the smaller golden rings already beginning to give off heat and crawl with rainbow sparks.

The smaller ring, Baby Bear, had moved on an arm made of living metal so that it was positioned inside a larger ring, Mama Bear, which also was warming up. Two spheres were going to form, one inside the other. What that meant, I had no idea, but I assumed Nakasu knew what he was doing.

Nakasu threw the flail to Penny and shouted.

Abby said to her, "He wants to know if you can work the coil, Mistress? Ilya cannot."

Penny did not look happy. "I know the basic settings. Wild Eyes lets me withstand the twilight for a short time."

"He says the settings are mated to the coil before which you now stand. Touch them not. He asks if you have your cap? He must form the aperture with you already inside it."

Penny looked shocked. "How does he know of my art?"

Abby repeated the question to Nakasu, but he was bent over the brass levers of the huge clockwork machine, throwing switches and spinning dials as fast as an epileptic playing *Flight of the Bumblebee* by Rimsky-Korsakov on a seven-keyboard pipe organ.

I took the sacred, ancient, unreplacable relic-beating crucifix from around my head, whirled the string of beads like David the shepherd boy warming up to smear a giant, and threw them to Foster. One more thing to confess to Father Flannery when I get back home.

He caught them. I said, "I want to know if you can work the crucifix."

Foster shrugged. "We followers of Odin can withstand the talismans of the White Christ for a short time. Didn't your god and mine both hang on a tree? Um..." He looked at the ivory and wood figure thoughtfully. "Where is the *on* switch?"

I said, "Remember! Roddy McDowall is wrong! Anyone can drive off a vampire with one of these! You've got to believe that!"

Foster said, "So you want me to have faith in the idea that I don't need to have faith for this to work?"

"Just stay frosty and keep the girls safe."

"Frosty Foster!" He made a snappy three-fingered Boy Scout salute. "That's me."

4. DECAPITATION

A window or hatch in the dome snapped open at that moment, and I saw a bald man, pale as a worm from a grave, with a long, drooping mustache like a biker—or maybe like

Fu Manchu—lean in and turn to look at me. I don't remember what his eyes looked like because when he looked at me, those eyes seemed to swell and envelop me. I was in a very cold, dark place, and I could not move a muscle or draw a breath.

I don't know why he struck at me first with his mesmeric power. Maybe it was just greed: I had the most life-force or whatever, so the leech latched on to me first.

Dimly, like it was something I was seeing through the wrong end of a telescope, something happening to someone else, I saw myself fall to the floor like a puppet with its strings cut, banging my head hard enough to draw blood, which started streaming through the air, not back into the wound, but toward him, the Bloodquaffer. And I was pushing toward him, offering it to him, using my weirdbeard teleproprioception to yield it to him.

I *craved* him to drink me. My memory of that moment, when I was actually helping my destroyers destroy me, is something I would give anything to erase. But it sits in my mind and will stay with me forever, disgusting and degrading, as if my soul were crawling with maggots, as if I were stained with a stain nothing could wash off. You know what made it worse? It was so sudden. One moment I was me. The next moment I was mutton, eager to be supped upon.

Dimly, I saw the murder holes snap open. The Bloodquaffers beyond—there must have been dozens of them, a whole platoon—could not stick their heads through, but they could reach their hands through, and their cold breath could crawl from mouth to arm to finger, form long, dripping streamers of vapor, and reach with a dozen tendrils of strange white mist into the chamber, reaching toward sources of life and heat.

5. TRANSMISSION

Nakasu was grinning so widely that his mouth looked like a shark-toothed sawblade wrapping his hips. He casually leaned on a plunger next to him. One of the Moebius coils near the bartizan, occupying the same wall where all the murder holes were placed, flamed darkly into being and then whistled, shrieked, screamed, roared, and opened up a tornado.

Just a small tornado. Ossifrage and the others were already behind the tightly-closed garage door, which I hoped was airtight.

I don't know if it was smart metal, or some other mechanism, or just the air pressure, but all the openings snapped shut with tremendous force. The mustachioed Bloodquaffer busy eating my soul was leaning in, so he had his head snapped off as neatly as if sliced by a guillotine.

As I came to my senses, I saw the severed head, a crazed look of surprise in his unendurable eyes, now bouncing like a basketball down the far wall. Did I say a basketball? It bounced like a watermelon filled with mercury.

The other dozen lost hands and fingers. Every opening now had a long smear of silvery white material like drool on a baby's chin after a messy feeding.

Nakasu, grinning from hip to hip, turned a wheel and shrunk the aperture to something smaller than a ping-pong ball. Keeping the air pressure lower than outside would make it almost impossible for the Bloodquaffers to open the doors.

Blue-white light blazed in the chamber. I assume there was some control or magic spell that brought up the gate-shutting light automatically during decompression disasters. Come to think of it, every gate I had seen had been in a room lit with lampwood or paved in lampwood.

Nakasu reached back and flicked the plunger back up, and the ball vanished.

Now I will say something you won't believe. Nakasu took out a whistle from God knows where and stuffed it in the blowhole between his shoulders, and then he did a jig.

I kid you not. A jig. He put his hands on his hips at the corners of his mouth and, neat as you please, hopped from one hippo-foot to the other, bending his legs in a kick-step. All the while his blowhole tooted and hooted through the whistle and a made a happy cacophony. It was a jig of joy.

Then, he noticed he was not alone. Since his eyes were not on a conveniently swivel mounted skull bag like mine, he had not seen me fall. He halted in shock, or perhaps in embarrassment, pointed toward me, and shouted something through his blowhole. Or tried to. Since the flute tube was still in his neck hole, all that came out was a note three octaves above high C.

Nonetheless, I got the message. The Moebius coil behind me had formed a black ball which was bigger than the hoop of the coil, enveloping the place where Penny had been standing. It was not making that teakettle whistle I was used to but was instead making a gargling sound. I could hear something rushing down the Coilpath toward me, something that was about to explode into the space where I was standing.

Penny was gone. She had been standing on the far side of the hoop from where the tornado formed in the gate across the room, so the suction had yanked her into the black sphere of our gate. It was neatly done. Nakasu was some sort of master at gatecraft.

Just so you can picture this correctly, Baby Bear ring and the black sphere it was emitting were invisible, entirely engulfed in the black sphere Mama Bear was emitting, which, unlike every Moebius coil I had seen before this, was also larger than the gold ring holding it.

Three things happened at once. One was that I jumped headfirst toward the black ball and reached out with my hands toward the last spot where I had seen the twisted golden hoop of the Moebius coil. The second thing was that the black sphere being emitted by Mama Bear swelled up to twice its size so that I was inside it almost before I jumped.

The third thing that happened was that I was struck with a solid piston of roaring force that must have broken every bone in my body.

My next-to-last thought before I lost consciousness was how glad I was that I was not only unkillable but that I could shake off the effects of multiple compound fractures the way other men can dust off a knee skid. Real glad.

My last thought was that I was rushing down a tube made of nothing which stretched indefinitely through a place that was not in any universe, but not in the now-familiar black nothingness of Uncreation. I was neither here nor in the Somewhither. I was Nowhither.

3

THE DELUGED WORLD

1. NOWHITHER

I am going to try to describe this, but it was weird, so bear with me.

I could not breathe. Some fluid that was not the Oobleck of Uncreation was tight around me, carrying me down like a mouse caught in a firehose.

I felt the weirdbeard sensation, that prickling of horror, that rage which told me it was time to kill or die, which announced the approach of another Undying. He was near, just above me. And there was another beyond him and another. They were all chasing me, like a line of paratroopers.

There was enough Oobleck in the well down which I fell that when I concentrated and called for light, light came: it was weird and reddish and grisly, but there was light—little fiery sparks of it.

I could see a thing that was roughly humanoid tumbling above me, red as a tomato, a dripping mass of gore not twenty feet overhead, and his arms and legs were twisted at impossible angles.

And there was another beyond him, smaller, and another beyond him, even smaller.

Panicked, I said a prayer to Saint Stanislaus Kostka and forced my broken bones whole, so I could try to move and draw my sword. The bone ends scraped together, and I screamed.

He screamed at the same time. I drew the sword. The line of Undying did the same thing. The exact same thing. Then, I noticed he was no longer red. Nor was I. He was dressed in my dad's Kevlar jacket. He was trying to draw my granddad's Japanese katana with the same motion. He was me.

I kicked my legs and rotated. Below me was a black dot that swelled up like a balloon. I struck and passed through the surface without any sensation. Inside was another black dot, also swelling up. It swelled, and I passed through its surface as well. I felt like I was stuck inside an endlessly growing Russian doll.

Of course. The black sphere formed by the Moebius coil is only black from the outside, where the photons fall in and do not bounce off and come out. You cannot see in. But the inside of the black sphere can let photons in, so you can see out. Instead of seeing a distorted image of the world that I was heading toward or heading from, I was seeing a distorted image of me.

Nakasu had placed the Baby Bear gatesphere inside the Mama Bear gatesphere. But the inner sphere was focused on the outer sphere, so each time I fell through the outer wall of the inner sphere, I came out again at the inner wall of the outer sphere. The lightwaves did, too.

I waved my hand in the medium and tried to draw a breath. Neither attempt worked like it would have done if this were air or Oobleck. I was underwater. The pressure was immense.

Nakasu had figured out a technique for opening a gate from a low pressure area, at less than one atmosphere of pressure, into a higher pressure area, without letting the entire high pressure environment explode into your departure point: put one gate inside the other and use them as airlocks.

I was now between the two spheres, in a place that was no place, and it was filled with water. Knack was probably admitting water into this nowither space slowly until it matched the pressure of the destination world. Then, Nakasu would flip a switch, disconnect Baby Bear from Mama Bear, and connect to the ring on the destination world.

On second thought, I doubted he had figured it out on the fly. If the Dark Tower had enjoyed this technology for three thousand years, every nuance of how to open gate spheres into vacuum and ocean bottom and mountaintops would have been discovered generations ago. Or, given their crazy setup, it could be future discoveries merely foreseen and instituted generations ago. It would be something so basic that they would not hesitate to teach it to underlings and slaves.

Cold like ice pierced me from all directions. It was freezing.

I wondered why I had not seen an image of the world toward which I was moving. Then, my ears popped as the pressured changed, and I went blind.

Ah. That explained it. I had been seeing the image of the world toward which I headed: an absolute black. There was no light in the world into which I came.

"Where am I?" I said, not expecting my lungs and mouth, full of ice water, to be able to make any audible noise.

Unexpectedly, I heard Penny's voice, crisp and clear. "We

are at the bottom of the sea, below the continental shelf, in the abyss where no light is. Even my people do not venture down so far."

What had Nakasu called it? The one unwatched coilpath. Anyone who was not a Sea-witch like her or Undying like me passing through this gate would die instantly. No wonder no one was watching it.

2. ANIMAL MAGNETISM

I saw a soft, sweet, pale light, but the weird thing was that I saw it with my mind before I saw it with my eye. I'm not sure how to explain it, but it was like this warm glow touched my skin, except I felt it not with my flesh, but inside my nerves, as a sensation of pure pleasure.

The water grew warm. I was no longer freezing.

I turned my head and saw Penny. Her ivory skin was afire with an inward glow, pulsing with passion. Her lips were parted, her head was thrown back, and her hair was a golden cloud in the water around her.

For a moment I thought she was nude, and I would have choked on sheer lust if I had not been choking on seawater already. But no, the light from her skin was shining through the translucent fabric of the thin white shift she wore, making her seem more nude than nude.

With an effort, I tore my eyes away. It did not help. I could still somehow feel the sensual warmth her body was shedding, almost as if it were driving directly into the pleasure center of my brain. It was maddening, hypnotic, magnetic.

It bothered me. Was I a man or not? Was I going to be run by my mad hormones my whole life, or was I going to man up and show some self-control? I was not that pleased with my recent performance, frankly. I had kept my word to

Penny and saved her, but broken it to Vorvolac and nearly gotten everyone killed. Everyone else, that is. Not including me.

No, I was not a man. I was an unkillable horror. I had control of my flesh and blood. Why couldn't I control my fleshy desires?

So I concentrated on the warm mesmeric sensation rippling through me. The wet, warm, and glowing girl in a see-through shift was making my heart race and my head feel light. I tried to block or undo those physical sensations.

As I always did when I had to concentrate, I said a prayer. *Saint Philomena, Behold me prostrate before the throne whereupon it has pleased the Most Holy Trinity to place thee... sustain me in suffering, fortify me in temptation, protect me from the dangers surrounding me, grant me the graces necessary to me... such as some goddam self-control! Oh, uh, sorry about the goddam part. Please edit that out.*

A sharp, biting, clear sensation—as shocking as plunging into an icy mountain stream—ran through me at that moment.

Maybe you don't believe in miracles. Maybe what happened inside me was just the residual Oobleck left over in my bloodstream reacting to the pressure of my will and altering my blood chemistry and neural reactions and hormone levels.

Maybe.

Or maybe Saint Philomena, who was thirteen years old when she decided to face torture and death rather than let an emperor take her virginity, was sitting on some white throne in a somewhere far above, with her face serene and innocent and pure, looked down, and saw me ogling and slobbering over Penny, so she stabbed something holy yet terrible into my boiling and lustful blood to help me out. You can make up your own mind about that.

All I know is that I could feel something like ice water in my veins—if ice water were electrified—and my brain seemed cleared of some of its fog.

3. THE DROWNED ATRIUM

Now I looked around. I saw her pale light reflected from the face of some blank-eyed, square-bearded king in a tall, cylindrical crown. The gold of this statue had not rusted away, but some dark growth that looked like worms turned to granite was growing from his cheeks and crown, his wings and bull-flanks. To his left, also written in gold and overgrown with dark, worm-like coral tubes, were murals of cuneiform.

More statues loomed beyond: dragons, falcons, serpents, and kings, all staring blind-eyed at nothing, all more patient than eternity. The place was about half the size of the main concourse of Grand Central Station.

I saw a row of two-story tall clockwork calculation machines just like in the atrium we had left, except these seemed like simpler, cruder models. Any part made of iron was rusted to nothing, so the golden gears and dial-faces were hanging alone or had fallen.

I was expecting to see seaweed and fish. Apparently, we were below the level where such things can live. The only fish I saw in the chamber were a group of translucent eels with eyes large and blank as ping-pong balls and teeth like clusters of needles. They fled from the light Penny shed, but I could see them gathering in the blocky shadows behind the pillars, glinting with an earthworm glow of their own. There were other creatures gleaming like ghosts in the shadows: crawling worm-like things or jellyfish small as coins and invertebrates made entirely of thorns and spines.

The chamber was square, rather than octagonal, and the tracks were made of bronze rather than living metal. The ceiling was flat rather than domed. The crowns on the statues seemed not to be as tall as their counterparts in the atrium we'd just left behind. The decorations seemed simpler: more natural, less stiff, less formal, with fewer decorations.

There were a dozen other Moebius coils in the chamber. All were made of gold and silver so were tarnished, but not rusted. The one behind me. I had come through. It was active, a dark ball surrounded by a very slight flicker of peacock-colored sparks. I could feel concentric waves of pressure coming off it. A solid sphere of water was expanding, pouring out from it, in order to push me into the chamber. Even as I looked, the ball vanished, and the inflow of water stopped.

I said, "Where are we?"

Penny said, "We must seal this room and pump in air. But the headless giant—what is his name?—thrust me here without explaining! I cannot work the living metal of the pumps and valves, even if any still exist in working order! What did he expect us to do?" Her voice was shrill, worried, maybe frightened. "Bloodquaffers can survive this place and follow us."

She had drifted near me, so I reached out and put a calming hand on her naked shoulder. The glow of her skin seemed to jump through the bones of my arm, go down my spine, and straight to my groin. Fortunately, that icy sensation was still cold and clear in my blood, and I resisted the impulse to grapple her and kiss her then and there.

Instead, I gritted my teeth and spoke calmly and firmly. "My dad always says in any emergency, to count your resources first and look to see what can be used, and used in a way you might have overlooked. Can you, I dunno, lend or loan someone your power to breathe water?"

She flinched at my touch and said, "Look out! Or you

will..." But then she stared at me, surprised, and, for some reason, glanced down at herself.

There was a lot to look at. It might have just been way the shadows fell, or the folds of her tunic, but her waist seemed slimmer, her curves rounder, her legs longer, her skin softer, and her lips so red they seemed to be pulsing with warm blood. But something in my cold blood told me that what I was seeing was not real.

I took my hand away. I said, "Kaqqudu Nakasu. I call him Knack."

She looked at my hand in surprise. It was almost a look of admiration. But all she said was, "Yes, to any I kiss, I can grant others the blessing to breathe water and withstand the cold and pressure, but only two. Three at most. Not a hundred."

Distracted, I said, "You kissed all those harem guards you killed?"

She gave me a dark look, and her skin shined brighter. "I am a siren. I kiss a lot of people. Few survive."

"Never mind. Let's focus on the task. If you open the gold flail into the Uncreation, will the water run out? Or will *ylem* run in?"

She again looked surprised. "I—I don't know. Adramelech is the only one who knew such stuff."

"*Ylem* reacts to thought. I made some into light just now. Could we make it into air?"

She looked at me sidelong. "You are the only one ever to have survived the Uncreation. You probably know as much about *ylem* and how to manipulate it as Adramelech."

"Who?"

The puzzled look vanished, and her normal expression returned. She rolled her eyes. "Professor Dreadful. The man who pays you to empty the trash and wax the floors?"

I said, "Use the flail. Open a small aperture into the

Uncreation, small enough so you and I are not sucked in. From what I saw, there do not seem to be consistent physical properties there, so things like pressure differentials may be... optional. If I can make Oobleck into air by prayer and willpower, why can't I make it into a high enough pressure air to drive the water in this chamber out?"

"This is the abyssopelagic zone. We are at three hundred atmospheres of pressure at least. Maybe four hundred. My cap protects me. I am not sure why you are not crushed into a lump."

"Clean living and cursed planet of origin," I said. I looked at the four dark walls of the vast windowless chamber again, the mud on the floor, and the glowing worms and creepy lamp-eyed eels with see-though flesh. I did not see any obvious openings. Would the air leak out? The Ur-men might build sturdy structures, but how sturdy? If this place was filled with one atmosphere of pressure, would it simply implode like a submarine below her depth?

The mental image of vampires breaking into the atrium chamber in Javan, where the hundred and fifty girls were cowering, and eating their souls in a sharklike feeding frenzy tormented me.

"Time is short. Let's try it." I said.

She put the flail on the muddy floor of the atrium, twisted it in the circle to make a hoop, and fiddled with the gold and ruby rings circling the haft for a moment. A pinpoint of darkness, almost unseen in the center of a sphere of multi-colored sparks, formed in the middle of the golden hoop.

A black pinpoint opened up to something small as a pea. I did not see any swirl like a bathtub drain produces or hear the teakettle whistle air leaking through small holes into the Uncreation makes, but when I put my hand near it, I felt a powerful current in the water, rushing toward the black spot.

She said, "How can we tell if this is working? How long until this room drains?"

I said, "Let me see. If we use the formula for the surface area of a sphere and assume three hundred atmospheres of pressure are pushing inward in all directions on that spot, and we take the cubic volume of this chamber and calculate how much water is coming into the chamber... um... let's say this room is sixty meters on a side, and the hole into non-space is three millimeters in radius... so... four pi radius squared... "

She said, "What do you get?"

"A headache. But maybe we are in a fantasy movie, not a science-fiction movie."

"What does that mean?"

"Fantasy means less math. I can feel the Oobleck beyond. Maybe I can coax it here. Who is the patron saint of air pressure?"

She looked at me as if I were crazy. Which proves she is a good judge of character.

Without speaking aloud, I recited:

As down in the sunless retreats of the ocean
Sweet flowers are springing no mortal can see,
So deep in my soul the still prayer of devotion
Unheard by the world, rises silently to thee...

A twilight effect like a sphere of shadow spread out from the aperture, and Penny's lovely light grew weaker. The weirdbeard sensation where I could sense the location of severed body parts was tickling me again: I could feel the Oobleck beyond the Moebius gate, swirling and storming, flopping and dancing, raging and splashing and crawling.

...Virgin all excelling
Mildest of the mild
Freed from sin, preserve us
Chaste and undefiled...

I was trying to make the dark, chaotic stuff want to be air and rush in through the aperture against the water pressure of three hundred atmospheres. But as I focused my thoughts in prayer, the icy, buzzing, electrical sensation in my veins seemed to reach out, invisible and impalpable, of its own accord, and touch the dark storm.

...*Mother of Christ, Star of the Sea*
Pray for the wanderer; pray for me.

As I talked, that cold, clear, and icy electric charge in my veins seemed to grow stronger.

The *ylem* was listening. It was like it was part of me.

I pulled it through the hole into here.

A sphere of dark, roiling fluid like mud with arms of darkness expanded out though each hemisphere of the opening, and, before I could think or speak, it changed and turned into a bubble of air that exploded into a thousand bubbles, and suddenly there was a storm of wind in here. I was puking water and was thigh-deep in the sea, but my face was in the air. The air was clinging to the ceiling and beating back at shivering walls of seawater.

Penny widened the aperture, increasing the surface area, and a hurricane stepped into the room. The seawater was driven back. I could hear no singing in the raging noise of wind, but I assume Penny sang some enchantment to change the nature of the water to make it willing to leave: at three hundred atmospheres of pressure, this dark water of the abyss was practically a different substance than the seawater of the surface—cold as ice and dense as metal.

I shouted to Penny, "Can we bring the others through?"

She shook her head and said something back I could not hear. But I understood: the air pressure was too high.

I am not sure how many atmospheres it would take to crush a man like an empty tin can, but I knew from my Dad talking about his scuba diving to know that the oxygen mix has to be adjusted the farther down you go in order for your lungs to work. Even for professional divers there are outside limits beyond which human lungs are not strong enough to push against the surrounding water pressure.

So how could I make this room a safe place to bring everyone? I confess to feeling a little panicky. There did not seem to be any solution, and I had no idea what Knack had in mind even though he clearly knew we were heading into an underwater environment.

Then, I saw the holes in the walls. They were small, about the size of the ring formed by your thumb touching your forefinger. There were fifty of them, but only ten or so were open. Water was pouring in, or, I should say, shooting in like machine gun fire. Imagine a firehose strong enough not just to knock a rioter off his feet but to cut him in half. But the holes were small and few and formed a straight line near the roof; these were the murder holes whose shutters had not shut.

The only thing I had in mind was the little Dutch boy. I was not thinking because if I had been, I never would have tried it. But I climbed up the dripping, tubeworm-crusted gold face of some dead king and stuck my finger in the hole.

Of course, it was like sticking my finger into a stream of machinegun bullets. Blood, bone, and mess jetted out of the hole, turning the stream red. My hand simply disintegrated, and my arm was broken under the shock. However, the pain made my body try to snap back into its normal shape, whereupon my hand reintegrated. Now it was stuck halfway through the hole, pinned at the wrist. I could not move it in nor out.

But I could, just by thinking, make my bones grow out through my knuckles and fingertips and form a solid shell. Then, I cut off my hand with my grandfather's katana. I had to make the blow sharp and swift enough that there was little pain so that my fist of solid bone would not revert to its true shape again, thus unplugging the hole.

Penny screamed.

I said, "Something wrong?"

She said back, "No, I... you startled me."

Rather than wiping the blood off my blade, since it was my blood, I just ordered it to jump back to my wrist stump. I reformed my hand so I could grip the sheath while I sheathed Dancing Maiden.

I inched my way across a gold set of clamps holding up a cuneiform plaque to reach the next roaring hole.

Remember those yards and yards of hair that were growing out of my skull? Well, for some reason, they did not return to normal when the shock of pain from losing a hand jarred me.

I saw no reason why, if I could make blood drops fly through the air at will, I could not fly my hair, even against a force of superdense water pressure.

I ordered a few strands to worm their way in around the edges of the hole. My hairs moved and writhed like snakes listening to a snake-charmer's flute. In they went, one by one. Each thread was so narrow in cross section that the water pressure did not eject it. I added a few more strands, then more and more, until the mass of hair on the far side was sufficient: and I turned that to a solid bone lump as well. And cutting off a braid of hair cost me no pain at all.

I was even smarter on the next try. I fed my entire head of hair in through the little hole, cut it off, and then asked the hairs from that side to seek and form lumps to plug the other holes in the line.

The sudden loss of noise was like going deaf. The water was no longer coming in. Penny was still glowing like a candle, but now she was standing hip-deep in cold water, not floating, and the translucent wet tunic was clinging tightly to her figure, emphasizing everything that was already emphasized.

I hopped down in to the muddy water. Little glowing worms beneath the surface winked like sickly stars.

To Penny I said, "As long as I concentrate, I can keep these holes plugged. Until someone arrives with Drain-O to remove clogged hair. How do we get the air pressure equalized?"

But I had forgotten Knack.

At the same moment when I asked the question, the black ball hovering in the center of the golden ring of the portable Moebius coil changed size and stopped emitting air. I could still dimly sense the Oobleck of Uncreation, but it was more distant. The color of the rainbows surrounding the black aperture also changed and grew steady.

I assume this meant Knack had tuned one of the Moebius coils on his side to the location of the portable coil and formed a hyperspatial tube. Then, I heard the air screaming, loudly at first, but rapidly growing quieter. Knack was using some sort of trick of the Moebius coil to equalize the pressure. Maybe he was just bleeding off the extra pressure and throwing it into the Uncreation through a valve, or maybe every Urrasse atrium had pumps or other gear to handle atmospheric differences.

I began to hear an ominous creaking and groaning coming from above and all around. I've seen submarine movies. It was not a good sound.

She turned to me. "Do you have a torch? I cannot let the others see me like this. They would go mad."

One of the items in my Dad's utility belt was a flashlight. The water pressure should have smashed it to flinders, but, to my shock and puzzlement, it seemed to be working just fine. A beam of bright light stabbed out into the gloom. "That is impossible! How can this thing still work? It must be made of unobtainium." I stared at the bulb in disbelief, momentarily dazzling myself.

I blinked blindly while she giggled.

"What's so funny?" I grimaced at the purple dancing spots before my eyes.

"Whenever I am tempted to overestimate you, you always do something to ground my opinion back in reality." But when I blinked again, she was just a normal girl, albeit more gorgeous than normal. She was no longer glowing; her lip redness and hip measurements seemed like they had been before.

I breathed in, expecting to smell salt and dampness. But instead I smelled the air of a warm and wonderful spring day. It smelled like a garden in which warm sun bathes perfumed air where soft breezes blow and lazy bumblebees hum.

"Wow," I said dumbly. "Did I do that? I make good air."

4. SUPERHUMAN POWER

I glanced over at Penny. Penny was standing on a toppled stone near a tablet of cuneiform set in the wall and held her hands near the writing. The water was around her calves, and the hem of her tunic was pasted to her upper thighs, down which thin threads of silver water ran.

Here I was, buried underwater, with no cold showers anywhere to be had. I tore my eyes away. I said, "Does it say where we are?"

"I can read only some of the words," she said. "It says the waystation is being sealed up until the rains abate. The date is over three thousand years ago."

I stared at the statues and at the layout of the room. "The Ur-men do not change their style of décor that often, do they?"

She said, "Since they can see in the future what their

descendants will build, innovation is unwanted. Children of astrologers want to make dress and architecture easy for remote great-grandfathers reading horoscopes to understand."

Another voice said, "The One are one across time as well as across space." It was Abby in her monkey-faced breathing mask, sitting atop the shoulder-line of Knack, coming out of the black sphere.

Ossifrage, meanwhile, came out from the top of the sphere.

Ossifrage winced as if he sensed something terrible. He strode through midair, cloak flapping, straight up to the middle of the ceiling. He tucked his crosier through his rope belt and placed both hands on the ceiling. His eyes were closed. I saw his lips moving.

The ominous creaking stopped.

Knack had a black wand in his massive hand, hooked on the end like a periscope. He flourished it and uttered something from his grinning waist.

Abby said, "The freedman says he is surprised you could make the far end life worthy. He had planned to merely set an anchor point here and stow the girl slaves in the nowhither space coils create between coils when they are nested. He compliments you by saying he thought the meatbag balanced on your shoulders where you keep your brain must be less flimsy than it appears."

I was still staring up at Ossifrage. I think he just saved our lives. I tried to calculate the weight of a column of water running to the surface from the bottom of an ocean trench.

I turned back to Abby and said, "Thank Nakasu for the nice compliment and tell him that I have freed the slavegirls by the authority of the One, True, Catholic, and Apostolic Holy Church, whose authority knows no boundaries but extends to all places when men are fallen and need saving. Tell him if he calls them slaves again, I will kick his ass up through the back of his impossible throat and out through his ugly teeth."

Nack hooted four harsh sounds and grinned even more broadly.

"He says that he could swallow your unclean, worm-like body at a gulp so that you would live in his bowels forever, for his excretion is mightier than you and would defeat you in the attempts to emerge. I believe he means this in a joking way."

"He said all that in four syllables?"

"His people have very curt and precise insults when it comes to eating and excreting."

She took off her breathing mask and pushed it back atop her head like a ball cap. The cheery monkey face was staring up at the ceiling Ossifrage held up.

That prompted me to ask, "How did you know it was safe to come through?"

She pointed at the black wand. "This instrument is a *balatuddnu usmekkum*." Lifeworthy-trial stick. "It tests destination conditions."

Knack shrugged her off his bench-shaped shoulder-surface and stepped back through the sphere. Abby said, "He goes to bring the rest. The Bloodquaffers gather outside the door, but not in numbers yet enough to slay; but the air is cold as the deadly northern pole."

Foster Hidden came through the sphere next. "Everyone safe?"

"Not for long. Ossifrage is holding up a zillion tons of seawater. We have to get out of here before he gets tired. Where is my crucifix?"

The girls began exiting the black hemisphere in all directions.

He said, "I gave it to Urad-Betti. The cute dark-haired one you talked to? Her faith in you was greater than mine."

I said, "But it is not supposed to work by faith. We've been through that. Christ drives back the vampires, not human belief."

Foster spread his hands. "When Urad-Betti picked up your *naudiz* rune, the little draculas beyond the door screamed and carried on. When I did, not so much. You explain it."

"What rune?"

"Naudiz. The rune of need. That is what a Christian cross looks like. Sort of."

"You learned that in Dark Elf school? Well, we are in need now. We only have a minute or two to find a way out of this deathtrap."

I told Foster to stand on the other side of the hemisphere of darkness. I drew my sword. I was expecting pursuit, but none came. Knack came through last, dragging a long chain behind him. Knack yanked the chain, and the chain stiffened, pulled itself from his hand, jumped into the black sphere, and vanished.

5. TRAPPED

The girls were squealing and carrying on, staring at the dark, half-flooded chamber with fear. They were not even as disciplined as a Boy Scout troop, who can be pretty squirrelly some times. I shouted to Abby to tell them to hush up and to form lines of five each. It was a quick way to count noses to see if anyone was missing.

Knack was smirking. I sheathed my sword, and with hand gestures asked him what that business with the chain Was. He made a pantomime motion as if he were pulling on a line and flipping a switch. He used his fingers to imitate walking along a path. He then mimicked the motion of taking the path in both hands and breaking it across his knee. And he grinned from hip to hip.

Urad-Betti came, knelt, called me master, and offered the crucifix back to me. I took it. "Get up!" I said. "I told you that you are free."

She bowed again. "I am happy to die as a free maiden."

I said, "No one is dying today! No one!"

Urad-Betti gazed up at the dark, dripping walls. The blank eyes of tall and inhuman statues glared down cryptically. Abby had ignited groups of cuneiform tables set in the walls, so we had a dim and yellowy light.

Some of the cracked and tilted platforms and piers were above water and coated with pools of mud. There were three large, square doors that were shut, which I assumed were cargo bays, and a large vault-door of bronze flanked with bas-reliefs of bird-headed hawkmen in pointed helmets.

Urad-Betti said, "This is a place of death. Some cities are commanded by the Ur to commit suicide, one and all. The ghosts are thick here."

I said, "Zip it. We are not going to be joining them." I turned to Knack. "Open one of these gates, please, and get us the heck out of here." I was looking at the strain on Ossifrage's face with growing fear.

Knack hooted and whistled from his blowhole. I heard him use the word *Istensehpgishur.* Since it was an Ursprache word, I understood it: *One-sided Circle.* It was their word for what Professor Dreadful called a Moebius coil.

Abby translated, "The Freedmen says the Moebius coils here lack virtue. They can receive a coilpath but not form one leading out. And there is no way to open the bronze door yonder into the sea without killing all in this chamber."

I said, "What if I opened the holes I patched and let the water into the main chamber here slowly?"

Penny said, "Slow or quick does not matter. It is four hundred atmospheres of pressure. I can protect myself and two others at most. But I could ferry us to the surface, two at a time, if yonder gate could be opened without the sea crushing the rest."

Nakasu coughed and asked a question. Abby said, "He asks how long to go from here to the surface?"

Penny said, "Between eleven and fifteen minutes one way, depending on the depth."

I said, "What about the bends?"

Penny said, "What is that?"

Abby said, "He means *the bends*."

When Abby said it, Penny heard it in her own language. Penny looked at me in surprise. "The secret of preventing dissolved gas from coming out of solution in one's bloodstream during decompression is part of our lore. This gas is..."

"We have carbon dioxide on my world," I said curtly.

Abby, for some reason, smothered a snort of laughter.

"What?" I said to Abby.

"Nothing," said Abby. "I was reminded of talking to you. I am unable to deduce what called this errant thought to mind. Please go on."

Penny said, "I can protect people from all the powers of the sea, including the bends. But, as I said, without my talismans, only two."

Nakasu scratched with his stick in the mud and goggled one pectoral eye at the result. Abby translated. "One hundred fifty-five passengers at four per hour is thirty-eight hours, forty-five minutes. Add in time to rest between each trip, almost two days."

I mused. I said to Penny, "I doubt we have two minutes, much less two days. You and I can carry everyone out at one go."

Penny looked doubtful. "How?"

I pointed at Knack, "He turns on the portable coil and throws it around one of the working gates here—one that can receive but not send. Then, he stows everyone inside the nowhither space of the coilpath. See? The coilpath bends in a loop, and you all just fall down it, round and round, perfectly safe. I carry the flail, with the gate active, to the surface. Easy-breezy, nice-as-you-pleasey."

Abby said, "Much of what the Freedman says is technical, and I cannot follow it. But it seems a nowhither gate, a gate leading back to itself, could indeed be erected using the portable coil and one of these fixed coils, but a switchman must stay behind here to undo the fixed gate manually to have any passengers or cargo held in the nowhither emerge safely at the portable coil. The Freedman says he must remain behind and perish."

Everyone looked stricken at this, and even some of the girls cried out softly in dismay. I felt proud of the ones who felt sorrow for him. I like any girl who overlooks how monstrous a guy looks. Guys almost never do that to girls. Go figure.

But I did not look stricken. I laughed a laugh of contempt, that awful laugh I have. It sounds terrible, but it kind of jumped out of my mouth without asking.

"Tell him no one is perishing today!" I said in a cross voice. "No one gets left behind! Ilya the Barbarian has spoken!"

4

SKULL MOUNTAIN FORTRESS

1. THE VOW

*A*bby repeated that to the group, and most of the girls looked puzzled. I wonder how the word *barbarian* translated in the various languages of worlds that never read Robert E. Howard.

Knack spoke again. Abby said patiently, "The Freedman explained to me that one of these fixed coils must be readjusted to a different diameter once the portable coil is on the surface. The outer surface of whatever coil is carried while active through the water must be adjusted so as not to admit water into the nowhither. On Javan, he had three working coils, whose relative diameters he could adjust to force changes in air and water pressure and prevent ..."

I said, "I am not leaving him behind! Everyone makes it home! Ilya, the Great and Powerful, has decreed it!"

That time, when Abby repeated my comment, some of the girls looked hopeful. Either that translated more easily, or they had read L. Frank Baum.

Knack spoke. Abby said, "The Freedman says someone must stay. It cannot be the sea-witch, for she must bring the portable coil to the surface, and it cannot be you because you are too stupid to learn the control settings."

"Stupid?"

"His word is bag-headed. Your head is like a bag."

I stared at him. "Are you suicidal, Knack? The solution is obvious."

Knack said something in a grinding, angry voice, which Abby translated. "My wish was to discomfort the Dark Tower. More than I dreamed was done: I saw the Lord of Magicians shamed,\ and the Great King thrown from his feet onto his rump. We have stolen one hundred fifty of the Great King's wives; the shame to him is beyond measure!"

I said, "That does not mean you have to die. What is wrong?"

Through Abby, Knack said, "My wife, my whelp, and all my precious things are now gone from my hand. The astrologers will torment them if it is foreseen this will cause me pain. If I am dead, however, the threat is no more. Why should I live? What is there for me on this world or any other? I have no kin on my homeworld; my mother gave birth to me in the Dark Tower while chained to the birthing bed, as her mother before her. Fate is fated: all things are written on the scrolls of the gods and sealed."

I said, "We can rescue your wife and kid."

Knack hooted from his belly-mouth and spread his huge, meaty hands at the dank stone of the vast, creaking ruins around us, the mud pools, and the waters in which blind-eyed eels swam. "*Ni hazina hii?*"

Abby did not have to translate. The tone of voice said it all. *For this?* Was I offering to rescue his wife and kid to bring them here?

I gritted my teeth. I said, "Abby, tell him he was made by

the high God, the highest God, the God above all other gods, the God who is above fate. Tell him the high God put into him the power of free will and wide-awake conscience, which places him above fate also. He has seen the Dark Tower cannot foretell his high acts, only his low ones. He is too precious to be left behind to die. He is the child of the high God, the beloved child. His life is sacred."

Knack laughed and spoke in a sardonic voice.

Abby said for him, "You speak madness."

I said, "My madness is cleaner than your sanity. Your sanity leads to despair, to death in a mud hole, which is madness; my madness leads to hope, which is sane. In any case, there is no time to debate!" I straightened my spine and threw my shoulders back, raising one hand high. "Abby! Tell them that I have taken a great and terrible oath, an oath I cannot break! You will all see your families again, see your homes again. Do the girls have people they left behind when they were kidnapped? We will work together. We will find a way home."

The girls looked suitably impressed. Even Foster was looking at me as if my words gave him heart. I said to him, "That goes for you, too, Foster! You have a home and family?"

He grinned a crooked grin and said, "Yes to the second. No to the first. You really think we are going to make it?"

I said, "Definitely. Abby, you, too."

Her voice was soft and shy. "It cannot be. My family has disowned me. My name is accursed. My home is your enemy. My mother is dead, and my father is no one. How could I ever see my home and family again?"

I said, "I do not know how. It is a high peak I can see rising above a misty valley. I know the destination. I don't see the best path there."

Knack, of course, understood her side of the conversation and looked grim. He spoke and spat a bucket load of spit from his belly-mouth. Abby said, "The Freedman doubts your strength."

"Tell him I will pray to the highest God, who has all strength."

Knack grunted. Abby did not have to translate. *What can he do?*

I spread my arms. "He has saved us so far. Do you think all these coincidences and lucky breaks are arranged by fate? Fate works for the enemy. We have something better."

"Better?"

I dropped my voice. "Do you remember the tale I told you? The one about the brave princess in a conquered country, when there was no room in the inn, so she gave birth to her boy in a stable, the prince who heals the sick and banishes devils? You said she must have been brave because that is the way princesses in tales act."

"I remember," She said. "He outsmarts lawyers and scholars when he is a boy. That was the best part."

I blinked in surprise. The best part?

It said a lot about the culture that reared her, I guess, that Abby thought it better to humiliate lawyers and scholars than to vanquish sickness or banish demons. Of course, in her world, such people were all astrologers, who all went mad living lives where they knew every day and hour as it was mapped out for them, and not a single decision was theirs to make for themselves.

I continued, "Well, we are part of that same story, you and I. My father works for the Vicar, who speaks for that prince and does his work on Earth. Each Sunday he appears to us, disguised as bread and wine. So his tale is ongoing, and you and I are part of it. His is a sad story, but it will have a happy ending, the happiest ever. Our part of the story might be sad like his, but it will have a happy ending, too. I promise. You are a princess, too, You have to be brave as she is. She is the Queen of Heaven, and all the angels bow to her."

Behind the lenses of her mask, I saw Abby's big, brown little-girl eyes get bigger and browner. They got little-girlier, too, if that is possible. A light of hopeful wonder danced there. She was trying to decide whether to believe me. Then, she dropped her eyes shyly and turned her head, so I did not see what the decision was.

I turned to Penny.

She raised a hand. "My nieces are insufferable, my aunts are overbearing, and my sisters are sly, so promise me no promises. I like your Earth better. Whatever we do, let us act quickly. I do not know how long Ossifrage can hold up the entire ocean."

And, for some reason, everyone looked at me.

2. THE PLAN

I smiled. I have a big bucktoothed smile and big yellow teeth like a horse, so I do not smile often. But at that moment, I had to. Finally, I understood why everyone, all these people who knew more than I did, or were older, or wiser, had been waiting for me to make the decisions. In an emergency, it does not matter who is barking out orders just as long as, first, it is one voice only, and, second, the voice has hope.

They had all been fighting the Dark Tower for too long. They believed in fate; it seeped into them. Their voices lacked hope.

Knack said, "And my wife?"

Through Abby, I said to him, "If you walk in the shadow of Abanshaddi and do deeds of a higher nature, the Dark Tower cannot see and cannot foresee. Would they torture her if they did not foreknow the result of that action?"

He did not look convinced, but he did not look stubborn

either. That meant he was convinced, at least in part, at least for now. It is easy to read expressions that cover the chest and stomach.

I raised my voice and had Abby repeat for me. "Here is our plan: Knack forms the nowhither gate, and everyone gets in it but four of us: me, Knack, Abby, and Penny. Penny protects Abby and Knack. Abby opens the living metal door. The sea floods in. We swim to the surface. I will wait there with the portable coil. Knack and Penny come back down here. Abby goes with so you can talk to each other. Knack works the control here to open my side of the gate, so everyone falls out."

Knack grunted. Abby said, "He asks how he lives while all this is done…?"

I said, "Penny kisses Knack." And I slapped Penny playfully on her shoulder. "Lucky you! Am I right this has to be a French kiss for the magic to work?"

Abby said, "Eew!"

Penny shot me a daggerly look. "A kiss on the forehead is sufficient, or, in the case of Nakasu, the collarbone above eyes."

3. BEYOND THE SHADOW

While Knack set up the flail and gathered the one hundred fifty girls into it, Penny turned to Abby and said, "Abanshaddi, can you read the writing on the walls here? What aeon is this?"

Abby looked at the golden tablets. She raised her hand, and a pale light shined from the letters. Some of the rows of cuneiform clicked and moved, opening additional cuneiform characters that had been hidden. Tubeworm growths were dislodged.

"This is Circassia, but the vulgar call it Thalassa, the Land of Sea. It is the home of the Circassians, who are the fairest of women. The Confusion of Tongues happened before the Great Deluge in this world because of the great evil of sons of Heaven taking as many of the daughters of men to themselves for wives, and from them came giants and the long-lived Cyrni. It says here that of all folk, these people were the most like unto the Ur, and hence it was most offensive that they refused oneness with the One. Here, more armies were brought than any other place since, for the giants were fearsome indeed and shed ichor, not blood, and drank soma."

I said, "Does it say more? Why was this place built under water? Is there a way out?"

Abby moved her hand. Rows of letters on the board above clicked into place.

"This place is called *Duhu Muhhumarut*." The word meant *fortress of the mountain-crown*, or it meant *skull mountain*. Which sounded like a base for a supervillain. Either way, it had once been on a hilltop, not a seabottom.

Abby read on. "The conquest was held in abeyance three thousand years ago, and this fortress was sealed and set aside because the flood waters crept up to the mountain peaks and swept all life away."

"Not all life," said Penny with a brilliant smile. It was the radiant smile I remembered from her newspaper photos. "For this is my world! My mother is from here."

"Can we call for rescue?" I said. "Radio for help?"

Penny shook her head. "We have no machines like radios. No fixed dwellings. Our palaces and houses float wherever the current carries us, and the flow of time is not the same in different levels of this sea. There are no landmarks. We have no toil, no farms, no mines, no wells, no shrines."

"How do you find each other?"

"We have whales send songs. Their songs can travel more than ten thousand miles. But whales never venture down this low. But it will not be hard once we reach the surface. Ossifrage can make the rest of you light enough to stand on the water, and I will sing to summon a whale." She laughed in relief. "Home! We are saved! We are beyond the shadow of the Dark Tower!"

Abby nodded but said sadly, "I rejoice you are at home again, Parthenope Seawitch. But the letters also say that when next Jupiter enters Virgo while Mars is in Aquarius, the waters will recede, and Ur will conquer this place. That is twelve years and a half."

4. BRONZE GATES

Knack also knew how to shorten segments of the portable coil after everyone was inside so that instead of carrying a hoop the diameter of a backyard wading pool, it was only about as big around as a manhole cover.

One clever variation Knack made to the plan was this: he connected the outer surface of the portable coil's sphere to the outer surface of the fixed coil we left running on the platform behind us. That way, instead of being forced to swim back down from the surface, Knack, Penny, and Abby could pop through the portable hole in one step, work the controls here to open my end of the coilpath, and let everybody out. Then, those three could swim back up.

He dialed down the diameter of the Moebius coil left running. It was smaller than a pea, almost too small to see. Knack said the water pressure emerging from the Moebius sphere on our side would be reduced to nothing due to the difference in surface areas.

Ossifrage was the last man into the black sphere. Knack made an adjustment, the sphere changed size, and the rainbow fires being given off changed color and texture. We four were standing in a circle. Abby had wound the chain of her kusarigama around the golden flail so that we could each hold our part of the portable coil without sticking our fingers into the black globe humming and burning in the center of the hoop. The globe was the size a beachball.

The walls and ceiling began creaking and groaning ominously. Penny placed Knack and Abby under her protection by kissing them—on the forehead, like a mother's kiss, you sicko—and I yanked the scattered parts of my body back to me. They turned to blood and sailed through the air and sloshed over me. I sucked my blood in through my mouth and nose, and a little in through my ears as well, and Penny wore a look of disgust on her face.

I secretly agreed with her, but since I would be dead a dozen times over without this particular power, I decided not to complain about how gross it was, not even in my own brain. Love ya', you gross power, you.

The holes those scattered parts had been plugging now shot firehoses into the chamber. It slowly filled up. Penny said, "I can remove the drowning sensation from the water as it goes over your heads. Breathe normally. Don't hyperventilate. Your lungs will feel heavier, and breathing will be a chore at first, but the discomfort soon passes."

The water when it lapped our ankles was bitterly ice cold, shockingly cold. Penny said, "As soon as you are breathing water, my art will adjust your blood chemistry, and the temperature will no longer offend you."

It was hard to hear her over the roar of the incoming water. Nack looked stoic and stolid, but Abby in her monkey mask was shivering. The water was soon up to our thighs.

I said, "The cold is too much for her."

Penny gritted her teeth and muttered something about "walkers" being too delicate.

There were square pits of stairwells leading to lower levels that were already filled. Without warning, Abby took off her mask and jumped into one of them. Penny cried out in alarm and dove after her. Knack and I, carrying the black-glowing sphere, stared at each other dumbly and did nothing.

Knack said something in an annoyed tone.

I don't know what he said, but I answered, "Yeah, you said it. What are they doing?"

The dripping heads of Penny and Abby emerged from the dark water at our feet. Abby said, "Sorry! But I was so cold. I thought if I started breathing water, the spell would take hold now, and I would be warm."

Penny said, "It is not a bad thought, but you must stay near me. At least within eyesight! There are ways to extend the charm, but I do not have the tools here."

I looked at Knack and shrugged. He grunted. We stepped down the first few stairs until the water was over my head and, a step or two later, over his shoulders.

I got to experience all the sensations of drowning and was chilled with the arctic cold, but Abby and Nack were fine.

As the chamber filled up, Abby and Penny, hand in hand, swam circles around us, giggling. Knack was floating next to me, with a worried look on his chest each time Penny was more than a yard or two away from him. My feet were firmly on the muddy stone.

Why they were buoyant when their lungs were as full of water as mine, but I was not buoyant, was one of those annoying things where the laws of nature seemed to be half-asleep, or had it out for me, or something.

But we could speak and hear each other normally. If anything, my hearing was sharper than normal, or the dense water carried the sound better than air.

I said, "Okay, gang. Moment of truth. If Abby cannot open the doors, we are stuck."

Abby looked worried. "Will we die?"

I smiled what I hoped was a comforting smile, but I probably looked like a circus horse drawing back his lips for a bite. "Little Sister, if we are stuck, we will figure out another way around the problem. Remember: you are foreverborn. Not even the stars know what you are going to do next, so you can never assume all paths are closed. Now try."

The doors creaked and groaned, popped and shrieked. With a long, slow, rumbling moan, the leaves of the doors drove inward, kicking up two clouds of flakes of rust and sea-mud, one to either side of the groaning doors.

Beyond were stars.

5. Strange Lights

For a moment, I stood there swaying with vertigo, wondering how I could be staring into outer space and wondering when I had lost my mind.

My eyes adjusted, and I began to see monsters among the stars, sleek dragons like frozen columns of twisting smoke and jeering goblins with faces round as shields. These vast, dark shapes must have been light years in length and stature, with grinning teeth and goggle-eyes larger than nebula, as if I were seeing them behind and above the stars of outer space.

I had been oriented as to person, place, and time up until I fell through a magic hoop lying on the grass out behind the Haunted Museum. The likeliest explanation is that I struck the storm-colored burning mud of Uncreation, and it entered my nervous system, and all the events allegedly experienced since, from the discovery of my immortality to the bloody fights, were nothing more than random nerve-firings going off in my dying brain, the wish fulfillment of a boy who wanted to do some heroic act before he died, but failed.

Then, I blinked and realized the stars were not stars, but the winking lights of deep undersea eels, skeletal fish made mostly of teeth, or distorted lamp-eyed creatures, all glowing like fireflies and glowworms. The dragons were decorations climbing the stones of a courtyard filled with the solid, dark, cold water of the ocean bottom. I also shivered, trying to drive morbid thoughts out of my head. Moms, don't let your kid read *Occurrence at Owl Creek Bridge*. His faith in reality will fail him when he needs it most: that crucial moment he discovers reality is a lot weirder than advertised.

I walked out of the gate, and Knack, carrying the other side of the black sphere, drifted with me. The girls swam out into the black courtyard, graceful as goldfish.

The yard was so narrow and long that it looked like a corridor. Onyx walls pressed in claustrophobically to either side, but there was no roof. Overhead were buttresses and archways, rotting but unfallen, whose capitals were carved into gargoyles. The goblins were gold monuments squatting on square stone pillars of basalt rising from the cold silt and mud of the floorstones. Some pillars had toppled, and some monstrosities were lying face down into the sea muck, as if the idols had quarreled and then tripped or pushed one another.

There was no light here save from the firefly-glow of skeletal, globe-eyed invertebrates. There was no sky overhead. Blind doorways and blind window-holes peered down from frowning walls of massive, cyclopean blocks.

The water was black as ink, cold as ice, and heavy as iron, and it reached to infinity in all directions. It could have been any hour of any season in any clime on the surface, noon or midnight, summer or winter, arctic or tropic; down here, we were buried alive.

6. Abyssopelagic

Off the muddy pavement we kicked. As we rose above the narrow black walls enclosing us, we came into a larger space with higher and darker walls. I kicked my legs frantically, and Knack made the motions of a ponderous dog-paddle with one hand and both stumpy legs.

The place was immense. We were like insects slowly drifting up between two nearly touching books on some giant's book shelf.

Finally, we emerged onto what seemed, at first, in the light shed from tiny transparent sea-worms, to be an endless black plain, with a cliff behind us and a drop before us. To either side were tall, crooked shadows and the glint of gold from coiling dragon-shapes.

There was an agitated motion in the sea-worm constellations around us. Brighter they grew. More and more luminous worms were gathering, and previously dim sea-bugs were lighting up their hooked teeth or snaky tendrils or globular eyes.

I froze, wondering what was happening. The other three stopped swimming.

In the new light, the crooked shadows to our left and right revealed themselves to be leafless trees of some species more gnarled and twisted of limb than any oak, taller than any sequoia. I wondered if they were dead, or mummified, or preserved by black magic from rotting in the sea from thousands of years past. Perhaps they were still alive, hibernating, awaiting the return of their masters.

We now saw we were swimming up from a crack between two balconies. The crack was huge to us but tiny compared to the acres of dark stone to each side. Each balcony was as immense as any balcony garden the Dark Tower itself boasted. These were the *kakkabillilkiritu,* the groves of the star-gods. For an aeon, no starlight had touched here, only the pale glint of luminous sea-worms.

Behind us, an immeasurable edifice, tier on tier, climbed up into the blackness. Before us the lower balconies formed a set of giant stairs leading vastly down and down.

Before it was drowned, it might have been taller than Everest from base to crown. You could have fit every major city on Earth inside it, stacked one atop the other, with elbow room to spare.

It was as if one of the stepped pyramids of Mexico had been built by engineers to whom the World Trade Center or Taipei Tower, or the arcologies or superscrapers that on my world were still pipe dreams and blueprints, would have been projects left for young apprentices.

As if...? Did I say *as if...?*

The Ur-folk had built this edifice. Compared to a structure that reached from surface to geosynchronous orbit, a mere mountain-sized building was a toolshed or a doghouse. The great Pyramid of Cheops would have been a doorstop, the Golden Gate Bridge, a handrail. What was it Professor Dreadful had said of them? *They are restrained from nothing they have imagined to do.*

The workmanship was the same as seen in the Dark Tower: rigid and regal figures of square-bearded king-faced bulls or stiff-winged minotaurs were here, sticking up into the gloom like the headstones of an abandoned churchyard or cobras with hoods of onyx and eyes of gold.

I hated the sight of them. I wondered if we were truly out of the reach of the shadow of the Dark Tower.

We were between two parallel rows of dead trees leading to the brink of the grove. More lights gathered as more insects were stirred up. Sea slugs and little spike-toothed fish began to emerge from between the boles of the trees. The thousands of shining worms and goblin-face fish and blind, ghost-like creatures like filmy scarves suddenly gathered as if a powerful current we could not feel were drawing them all together.

The lights swirled hypnotically inward to a wide circle facing us. The fish-things formed a hoop of lanterns just beyond the brink of the balustrade. A second ring of glow-worm lights formed inside it, parallel but farther off, made smaller by perspective: and a third and a fourth and so on. All the rings together formed a glinting tunnel leading out into the black abyss.

The sight of the nested rings reminded me uncomfortably of a staring eye, or perhaps of the ribcage of an invisible snake whose mouth was pointed right at me.

"Penny!" I said, "What is this? Is this something your people here can do?"

Her expression was nervous. She said, "I have cajoled dolphins and whales to cavort in circles to greet approaching guests in just such a cylindrical dance and beckon them closer. I can to do such tricks, for I studied under the theriomancers of Amorreus, as only our royal blood is allowed."

"Is it an invitation?" I asked. "So is one of your royalty at the far side of this tunnel?

"No. We never venture so far down. I have never heard of one of us taming anglerfish, night-worms, fang-tooths, or comb jellies."

"But your people can survive this low! None visit the sea-trench floor?"

She gave me an odd look. "None. You landwalkers bury your dead in solid earth and walk atop them, and the damned are pulled lower still, to the core fires. All our dead sink down. We swim above them, but they can still see us. Your hell has a roof. Ours does not. Why come here?"

The more distant little lights were circling and circling, one within the other. They looked like fairy lamps. It was charming and inviting.

But the nearest ring of glowing deep-sea creatures was close. I could see the wormy things that looked like famished wraiths with bulging eyes and skull-faces. All the fang-clusters and crooked needles protruding from their transparent hides and gaping mouths looked like torture hooks left behind by lazy Ur tormentors after the inquisition was done. The glow-fish looked a lot like ghosts, but not ones who made it to the good place.

"There is lots of gold down here." I said. "No treasure hunter ever drops by?"

"You sound like Eflast! It is a worthless metal, heavy and cold. Its power is of the sun. Ours is of the moon."

"No explorer?" I said. "No archaeologist?"

She said, "My sisters are light of heart. We don't meddle with things of long ago and far away. That madness only technomancer worlds possess."

"Or someone could have come here to meet us."

"But how could anyone know we were here?"

I said impatiently, "But if it is not one of your people, who can it be?"

Her eyes flashed angrily. "My world is two-thirds greater than yours in inhabitable area, for we dwell in all our seas and to three zones of depth. Much is unknown. My world is not tame, not safe. Twilight haunts the deep and is known to call monsters from alien seas hither. I do not know who sends this path!"

"Only way to find out." I looked at Abby. "Any objections? Knack? Abby?"

She had been repeating our words to Knack, who twisted his stomach in a wry smile and held up his free hand, wiggling his fingers. Abby said, "The Freedman says, on his right hand, if we float on the surface in the sun, without water, we will not live long, unless the sea-witches find us and succor us. On his left hand, if we follow this path of light to find whoever makes these fish dance, we will also not live long unless the sea-witches find us and succor us. He says the five fingers of one hand are not less than the five of his right but are the same." Abby smiled, "As for me, we are now in a world that is as strange to me as it is to you, Ilya the Barbarian. I have no counsel to give."

So off we went. They swam easily and swiftly, and I kicked and struggled and strained to force my non-buoyant body to keep up.

The lights led up at a steep angle. The vast stepped pyramid of the Ur sank into darkness behind us. On and on we swam.

5

CITY BENEATH THE WAVES

1. Slower Time Strata

*W*e followed the undersea road of glowing sea creatures. I sang a cheerful song until I ran out of breath right in the middle of *because of the wonderful things he does...*

Don't ask me how I ran out of breath when I was not breathing in the first place. The song died. The silence was deafening, the cold painful, the dark heaviness of the water maddening.

I gritted my teeth and ignored the pounding headache in my skull, the screaming ache in my muscles, and the heavy, choking sensation from my water-filled lungs. I just kicked my legs and kicked and kicked. Rahab, the other Undying monstrosity like me, boasted he had a technique to remove fatigue and ache from his muscles. Right then, I was really wishing I knew it. Every kick was torture.

After a time, the fish forming the path seemed less skull faced and clear skinned and looked more like normal sea creatures: bioluminous shrimp and squid, seaworms and jellies.

I said, "I thought it would only take fifteen minutes or so to reach the surface."

Penny was in her element. Her golden hair was a cloud like a comet's tail behind her, lovely even in the sick seaworm-light of the path we followed. She swam using a stroke I do not know the name of: with her arms back and her legs moving in unison, like the flippers of a dolphin. She said, "We are passing through a slower time strata of the water."

"What is that?"

But she did not answer, for she gasped, and a moment later, so did Abby. I was not able to see it in the pitch blackness until we were closer.

What came into view was a vast translucent orb, bright as a pearl. It looked like a bubble, and inside were burning lamps of silver, blue, and green fire, flicking and dancing. In orbit around the pearly orb were a dozen lesser pearly orbs, moving at different rates, also aglow with inner lights.

It looked like Jupiter with moons, but wrought in glass.

Silver tendrils that looked like rivers of air branched out from the central pearl to the smaller ones, and a connected ring of silver, like the rings of Saturn, circled the equator, connecting the larger moons. I saw lights passing up and down the silver threads of air. They might have been ships, or carriages, or priestesses in holy procession.

I saw one river of air disconnect from a moon-like lesser orb as it passed, sway like a tentacle, and grasp another. Not all the rivers of air were connected to orbs. Some were connected to each other. Through the hull of the great orb, I saw that there were also lesser orbs inside, and they were also connected to waterfalls, lakes, or streams of air.

The closer we came, the larger the orb appeared until the

lamps within the great glass pearl seemed like city light seen from the passing plane, like streetlamps and hearth-fires, and they cast the shadows of towers and bridges against the dome. The lesser pearls were like villages surrounding a walled town.

And music came from it, passing without echoes through the dense black ocean. Voices, sopranos and altos which were silver in the ear, poured out a wordless murmur, seductive, soft, slow. *Seee-kvaaarrr-u-looo!Seee-kvaaarrr-u-looo-ooo!*

The voice formed words.

> Siq'varulo, dzalsa shensa vin ars rome ar
>   hmonebdes?
> Vin ars romy gulsa t'akht'ad, okhrvas khark'ad
>   ara gtsemdes?

Closer yet, I saw that the great orb was very much like Jupiter. It had different bands of iridescent color, like the filmy rainbows seen in bubbles, rotating at different speed at different latitudes. It even had something that looked like the Great Red Spot: a glassy oval or swirl behind which many pink lamps were gathered.

I said, "Does anyone other than me hear those voices?"

> Sjulsa shensa q'vela erchis: beri, eri, mepe,
>   q'matsa;
> Khelmts'ipe khar tvitmp'q'robeli, t'akht'i mza
>   gakvs, hgieb satsa,

Penny was beginning to glow. Her face lit up. I mean that literally; her body shined with that radiance that bypassed the eyes and stabbed directly into the pleasure center of the brain. Her tunic turned translucent from the light beneath, and her body grew glorious to behold.

She threw back her head. It was achingly beautiful and made my heart stop and leap into the back of my throat at the same time. Parthenope—for she did not look like Penny any more, not to me—cried out in joy. "These are my sisters! This is the tongue of Circassia!"

"What are they saying?"

As the turning of the great orb brought the red lit spot closer to us, it opened, and a double line of lights swam out at an unhurried, dreamlike pace, coming toward us.

Parthenope said, "The song praises love as the divine power. Ah. It says… I am not sure how to render it… *Love, who is the power which of thee shall serve, with no will?*"

Abanshaddi said, "Permit me…" She chanted:

> O love! Thy power enslaves all hearts and all
> > creation holds in thrall,
> Monarchs bend to thee the knee, and on thy
> > shrine prostrating fall.
> Thy laws all overawe: priest or peon, overlord,
> > or archangel high;
> Caesar absolute art thou; thy throne, the dew of
> > ardent tear and sigh.

I now saw the twin lines were indeed nude and half-nude women, perfect in proportion, lovely in features, shining with a clear light. Each maiden swam in the cloud of her own hair, golden or fiery-red or black as night. Their long and shapely legs trailed after them. In their hands were little lamps which contained sparks of the light they themselves were shedding, but brighter. The weightless grace that ballet mimics, here, before my eyes, was real.

There are many things like this on my world: beauty contests, chorus lines of showgirls, actresses in pageants, girls dressed as bunnies in gambling casinos. But all of those where mimics, too, and fake. There was nothing like this on my world.

I have never been drunk, but I felt like my brain was swimming in wine.

> Shenis ughlisgan gamosvla net'a undodes
>   radme vis!
> Tu shen khar vnebis mizezi, lkhenats shengan
>   ar gvedzlevis?

Call them mermaids even though they had shapely dancer's legs. Each had something like a scarf of see-though fabric as her only garb. It ran from behind her neck, criss-crossed at her breasts, and passed around her back, was cinched tightly at the waist, and passed around the luxurious curves of the hips and then gathered again between her legs like a river delta leaving the whole sinuous length of thigh and calf bare. Unlike land beauties, trains nine yards long neither dragged on the ground nor had to be held by ladies in waiting. The folds of fabric swam after them like a long tail. Or, when I looked again, I saw the trains were undulating in the water, ripping like the flukes of an eel. These long serpentine scarves were alive and were propulsion.

Closer they came, swaying, sporting, swooping, swimming. If I had not been drowned already, I would have been unable to breathe.

> Namdvil k'etil ars gantskhroma, igi numts-odes
>   gvelevis,
> Masha tsudia, tu mashi sibnelets arsit erevis!

The song was now inside my brain as well as outside. I was hearing it with my ears, but it was also pulsing in my bloodstream.

Some thought, dim and weak as a fruitfly tapping against a windowpane, tickled me. What were the words? What were the women saying?

Abby was still repeating:

> Has ever fettered slave sought Exodus
>   from thee
> Or from the soaring sweetness of thy madness
>   to be free?
> This sin is holy, sweet, and fine; let all its
>   ecstasies be mine
> And I gladly die, forsaking sky, thy willing
>   slave, O love divine!

Then they were with us, among us, darting and laughing. One embraced Parthenope with girlish shrieks of joy. Others petted Abby and cooed.

And me: long, sinuous soft arms and fingers wondrously fair as branching coral caressed me here and there and tousled my ungainly hair. One of them wound her delicious arms around my waist, and a second teasingly kissed my thigh. Two and three, rightside up and upside down, peered quizzically into my face, eyes sparkling with mirth, lips half parted, scorching me with smoldering gazes, leaning in as if about to kiss my lips and then darting away, giggling. I remember one who pirouetted before me, her long cloud of hair a black banner winding around and around her white limbs, as she arched her back and ran her fingers through her hair, elbows high, one leg bent, the other curved in the arc her curving body made as she did a slow and sinuous back-flip through the water.

I felt a tingling sensation all over my body, and a warmth, from where the one mermaid had kissed my leg; as it turned out, that was enough because my eyesight was sharper, and my body was buoyant. It no longer looked gloomy to me.

Better yet, I no longer had to struggle and kick just to keep from sinking. I could feel my lungs working. Somehow they were drawing oxygen out of the seawater.

And my headache was gone. No doubt it had been caused by the bends and all the little gas bubbles causing strokes in my brain that would have killed a normal guy nine times over.

Sometimes it is good to be an invulnerable monstrosity.

2. The Great Orb

Memory and sense became a blur. I was looking at nothing but cleavages, smiles, hips, flashing eyes, and floating hair. I was hearing nothing but sinuous, sensuous, sonorous song.

Dimly, I saw we were now near the oval of pink lanterns, and the singing, playful Circassians were drawing us ever closer. I looked up at the silver valve of the Great Red Spot, which was open to receive us. Beams of colored light and strains of sensuous song spilled out to receive us. I felt warm, relaxed, and safe, as if my soul were wrapped in cotton.

The gleaming, semi-transparent wall ballooned outward and loomed toward us. A yard-wide circular opening suddenly gaped, stretching like molten glass. It was around us and behind us, and it snapped shut.

I lost sight of Abby and Parthenope. I should have been worried, but, then again, had we not been hoping exactly for this? To be rescued by Parthenope's people. They were the ones who had sent her into the Dark Tower, were they not? If they were the enemy of my enemy, that made them friends.

And the lovely, lovely, smiling girls who blew kisses at me and teased me and smiled and twirled and danced and gyrated and laughed such merry laughter certainly seemed friendly enough.

Near us, like a flock of birds, tiny bubbles of a brighter hue of air carried little lanterns made of coral or shell and burned with strangely colored fires. A particularly large dome was sailing directly below the puckered gate. The bubble that held us descended, passed through the walls of the dome, and brought us to a place that had no lights at all, merely darkness, music, warm caresses, laughter, scented perfume.

Soft arms encircled me. Someone soft and curvy who smelled simply wonderful kissed me on the lips. It was warm and sweet and electric. I hoped it was Parthenope. She handed me a wine cup and put it to my lips. I took a sip; it was brackish, like sea water, but before I could spit it out, a whirling dizziness filled my head, clogged my nose with stinging fumes, and made pins and needles of numbness crawl up my limbs and into my chest.

I knew I could not die, so I decided I must be asleep. Lights out.

3. Earthly Paradise Undersea

I woke to soft music of strings and flute and tambourine.

I was feeling obscurely foolish but was still buoyed by a tinkling, joyful sense of ebullience. It was like the time my older brothers decided to ditch me in Disneyland after Father had told them to keep a strict eye on me. On the one hand, I felt foolish for letting them fool me, but on the other, it was Disneyland. What better place for a little kid to get lost in?

But it was so comfortable here, so very comfortable. Silk and satin pillows were beneath me, soft and yielding, and scented with a musky and sweet scent, like ambergris.

When was the last time I had slept?

I took me a while to calculate backward. I may have nodded off while I was sitting in the dark and lost corridors after escaping from the ghost of the pharaoh who gave me the golden flail, just before Pallishabdu the Plumber found me. I honestly did not remember. But I had slept a little, standing up, in the bottle-shaped glass boat Abby and I had used to escape from my torture birdcage at forty thousand feet. But when had I last slept a good night's sleep, uninterrupted, without being speared by an iron wand of living metal?

Back in Albion, in Tillamook, Oregon. Of course, I had not slept well back then either since I prayed for the soul of my mother every night, and that always reminded me of how much I missed her. So it had been an eternity since I had slept a good night's sleep.

And I realized with a shock that I had stopped thinking of my world as *Earth*. In my mind, I had called it *Albion*. The enemy's name for it.

I opened my eyes and sat up. I was naked again. Of course. You'd think I be getting used to that my now.

Around me were bed curtains. I could smell food and wine. The music, coming from some hidden speaker, was a sinuous melody threaded through with a strange, hypnotic humming or buzzing flute while a tambourine pulsed to keep the beat. I was in what looked like a waterbed without any bed: a pond of liquid whose surface tension could not break was beneath layers of silk cushions. Scarlet and pink hangings depended from the dome above, and they were set with pearls and abalone. Little lamps held inside floating bubbles of water hovered here and there in the air. How they burned inside water, or how the water stayed afloat, I could not guess.

It took me a moment of floundering to stand up. The

floor was coated with sea lion fur rugs, or otter pelts, or something even softer, piled three deep.

I pushed the soft fur rugs aside with my foot and saw the glass-clear, shining substance beneath. It was ice, but it was warm ice. Room temperature. How the mermaids could change the melting point of ice, I could not guess.

No, hold up. Of course I could guess!

I remembered seeing Penny drown Rahab by putting a ghostly version of water from a bottle over his face and making the air behave like water. Her mermaid cap allowed her to do the opposite to Abby and Knack and to make water like air to them. So I could assume the mermaids could alter the physical properties of water. Or the spiritual properties? If the properties they could alter included buoyancy, they could make water light as air. And I was lying on a bed whose surface tension had been increased.

I pushed aside the pink curtains. The fabric was as smooth as oil and seemed to linger in my grip and caress my hand. It was so pleasant to the touch that it made all my hair stand up on my neck. I resisted the urge to rub the stuff against my face and chest.

I was inside a bubble of air the size of the tent of the sheik of Araby and decorated in something of the same fashion. The bottom third of the sphere was filled with ice to form a circular floor. The pink curtains slanting down from the zenith of the dome formed bed curtains like a teepee and hid what was on the far side of the spherical chamber from me. Cushions, pillows, and mats had been piled on the floor, and lamps, and a tripod brazier holding, not glowing coals, but a globe of floating water with a luminous fish inside. He gave me a cynical look with his overlarge globular eyes and grinned with what looked like a mouth full of white needles.

The sides of the chamber were transparent. The bubble-chamber where I stood was floating halfway up in a vast spherical space encompassing an underwater city. The city was dark, lamp-lit, mysterious, unearthly. My bubble was floating in a spherical lake, and the lake was floating in midair, without any support. Concentric bubbles to each side held either spheres of water or spheres of air. Some were connected by curving arches of water, some by tunnels of air. Circular shelves below held coral banks or tanks of bright golden fish. Larger bubbles of darker water held sea serpents and one-horned whales.

So wide was the great orb of the city that even these dark, spherical whale tanks were lost in the vast circumference. Large bubbles like clusters of grapes clung to fountains or waterfalls of white or blue-gray water rising or falling at the vertical axis of the great orb. When I saw through the walls slender figures being towed by dolphins in chariots shaped like shells through these midair bridges of water, I realized the insubstantial bridges were as long as boulevards, and the grape clusters were as tall as skyscrapers. It was not just a city but a vast metropolis.

But then I saw some bubbles leaving from the great orb, passing freely through the rainbow wall of air into the outer sea, and others entering. So the word city is not right. This was a caravanserai, a temporary meeting spot. The spheres and clusters of spheres were not like buildings but more like tents, or houseboats.

And all the gleaming spheres, orbs within orbs, were moving and rotating. I saw wheels turning within wheels, with spokes made of silvery rivers of air cutting through the waters. Don't think of a clockwork. Think of a dance.

But beyond the walls of the Great Orb was the darkness of the region of the sea where sunlight never comes and the pressure is hundreds of atmospheres. This was not the nice part of the sea where clown fish and manta rays slide in and out of coral beds as bright as jewels, with the tropical sun like a shimmering and dancing lamp shining through a restless, ever-moving ceiling. No, this was like something from another planet, a cold one, larger than Earth and less hospitable.

I pulled my eyes to the near distance. I saw a pair of half-naked women, as beautiful as dreams, gliding past in a tubular river of water held in midair, their arms about each other. They turned and waved, blowing kisses and beckoning. I looked, down, remembering that I was both ugly and naked.

Embarrassed, I turned and rounded the pink teepee in the center of the chamber, hoping to put something opaque between me and the lovely, laughing eyes of bathing beauties I did not know. I discovered the hard way that the icy parts of the floor were slippery, so I stuck to the sealskins and rugs.

On the far side of the sleeping teepee was an expanse of floor covered with pillows and rugs as soft as clouds and black as midnight. There were thirty or forty girls here, all asleep on the black rugs, their shapely limbs draped luxuriously across the folds and piled cushions of the floor. I could hear soft breathing, and one or two snored or turned and murmured in their dreams.

These were not glowing women adorned with supernatural beauty, but they were all young and cute. I did not recognize them at first because they had been fed and rested, and their resting faces no longer showed any sign of terror and despair. They had also all been given new clothing to wear—clinging silks and satin saris of citrine, rose, and lavender. After a moment, it dawned on me that these were the perfectly normal ex-slave girls I had just saved from the Dark Tower.

There was evidence of a feast scattered here: clamshells used as platters with fishbones left on them and mussel shells and tails of shrimp in a pile. I saw no bottles, but I did see globes and globules of green wine floating in midair and drinking vessels made from the horns of narwhales. It looked like the girls had feasted until they dropped. Or had been knocked out by drugs in the wine.

And there was not the right number here. This was only about a third of the whole of them. The busty girl with the snake body I did not see, nor the one I called Betty. I did not know any other of their names. (That made me feel less heroic. You are supposed to find out the names of the girls you rescue. That rule should be in the heroic handbook somewhere.)

There was a curtain on the far side beyond the sleeping women. I suddenly realized that the music was coming from beyond the curtain. Of course, in my life, I don't think I have ever heard live music outside of mass or campfire songs. So I had been assuming this was background music, a recording, or the radio. But they did not have radios here. Penny had told me so.

Even as I looked, the curtain grew transparent, becoming a sheet of water. It fell with dreamlike slowness to a part of the floor covered by no pelts and was absorbed into the ice.

4. All-Girl Band

Beyond saw four supernaturally beautiful seamaidens seated on a dais of shell. Three were playing the lute, violin ,and double-flute while the fourth beat a throbbing rhythm on a small drum she held at her shoulder. They were an auburn, a light brunette, a dark brunette; the drummer was a redhead with a mass of hair that fell to her knees. Their skin was shining but very dimly, mere whips of brightness clinging to their curvaceous, half-clad forms. They were dressed in filmy scarves that implied and exaggerated everything they hid.

A fifth maiden, facing away from me, was kneeling before them, and her honey-blonde curls, disheveled, cascaded past her supple spine and tickled her hips like wanton vines that escape the trellis. Her delicate feet were tucked beneath her rump, which was as shapely and pink as the cleavage of a peach. She turned and looked alluringly over her shoulder at me, smiling archly.

For a moment, I thought it was Penny wearing a honey-colored wig: but no. It was a strong family resemblance.

The honey-blonde was their living music stand, for she held up a book of mirrored pages toward them. I remembered seeing Penny with such a book: it was a spellbook, a grimoire.

She held the book in one hand and waved her fingers at me with the other, a hypnotic gesture. The music stuck a deeper chord, and the strings began to sing alluringly.

Behind the musicians was the clear glassy wall of the dome. Outside was water. In the water was a woman larger than a killer whale. She was perfectly proportioned, with exquisitely rounded hips, a waist narrow and supple at least in comparison to the rest, and breasts as round as the moon and fair as ivory.

Her face, despite its giant size, was delicate of mold, narrow of chin. Her lips were remarkably red and her teeth as white as the teeth of a sea lion, and her enormous long-lashed eyes regarded me with a cryptic and mesmerizing gaze. Her hair was dark as night and blending into the dark water all around her, so I could not see where one ended and the other began. Her eyes were dark, smoldering oceans in which the soul could lose itself forever. Her dark eyebrows curved just so, like the curve of a Japanese longbow, the *yumi*, which curved more sharply on one side than the other, and as large. Her skin as clear as milk.

I saw her once, that one time only. The image was burned into the hungry and animalistic part of my soul. I could describe her every feature in detail and would need to grope for words fair and fine enough to be worthy of the impossible task.

It was absurd that I should find such a monstrous, huge woman attractive, but she was perfect. And she reminded me of Penny. I recognized the slant of the cheekbones, the fullness of the lip, and the shape of the eyes.

I remembered then something Penny had said. "My mother cannot come up on land. Weight problems, you might say." No evidence told me, but nonetheless I was convinced that this immense and supernatural being was the mother of which Penny spoke.

The mother looked me over carefully and spoke in the language of the Circassians. I did not understand a word but the tone of voice was a command. She raised her shining and shapely arm and pointed.

Then, moved by some current I could not see, the oceanic titaness was drawn backward out of sight and was swallowed by the darkness of the water beyond the curving wall.

5. The Music of the Sea

I turned. What had she been pointing at? I saw the fountains and waterfalls that formed the central axis of the city, the clusters of bubbles like rounded skyscrapers, disk of ponds and seabed gardens. There was a larger sphere, bright as an opal, right in the center of the great orb, blue as a peacock's neck, surrounding by orbiting lights of indigo and heliotrope.

I jumped in surprise when soft hands touched me from

behind. It was the lutist and the drummer. They had slung their instruments, so the background music now was flute and violin. They were led by the fifth mermaid, the honey-blonde. She was carrying silken garments over one arm; the next held my father's Kevlar jacket; the final carried my father's money belt, baldric and scabbard, as well as my grandfather's katana, Dancing Maiden.

These three were shining with their bioluminescent clarity, which emphasized their allure, and sent a warm pulsing sensation directly into the pleasure centers of the brain.

The honey-blonde who looked like Penny knelt and tried to wind a loincloth around my loins. I was having some issues with my loins at that particular moment and was holding a pillow in front of my crotch, so it was rather awkward to try to negotiate away from the voluptuous woman of unearthly beauty attempting to put her hands on me.

The other two, the lighter and the darker redhead, stepped up behind me, hemming me in. They spoke in soft, cooing voices, sultry and sexy as all get-out, but I have no idea what they said.

Then, they tried to dress me. I was blushing, which amused them. "Listen," I said softly. I was speaking quietly because I did not want to wake up all the sleeping teenagers rescued from Ur. "I can dress myself. Thanks but no thanks. Me am big boy now."

I tried to pantomime my meaning with one arm. No good. The sea-maidens were now cozying up to me like pussycats trying to make friends. The auburn rubbed her cheek against my shoulder and whispered something breathy and urgent in my ear in a language I did not speak. The redhead wound her pale and shapely arms around me and whispered something in the other ear. The tone of voice was what one might use to calm a skittish stallion.

I took the redhead by the shoulder and gently but firmly put her at arm's length. Touching her shoulder had the same effect, but triply magnified, that touching the curtains had. It was electric. Now I spoke. Since they could not speak my language, I said, "A scout is trustworthy, loyal, helpful, friendly, courteous, kind..." but I said it in tones of command, as if I were older than these ladies.

She kissed my fingers.

I put my free hand on the elbow of the auburn and tried to urge her gently away, but that let the other two close in again. My tone became sharper. "Obedient! Cheerful! Thrifty!" I shooed and pantomimed for them to stand away.

The auburn and the redhead grabbed my arms in their sweet, lovely, soft little hands, and a struggle began. It was an uneven wrestling match because all the girls wanted to do was toss their hair and tease me, and I was trying to get away without hurting them or making too much noise. Their bodies were soft and rounded and warm, and they smelled wonderful.

Wrestling with girls is fun.

They sort of won the wrestling match. The musicians began to play a louder, faster tune. It filled my head like wine. My limbs were wrapped in a warm, floating feeling that was very pleasant indeed. My thoughts swam in a fog, and I lost track of what had been worrying me. Why not just get dressed like the pretty women wanted?

I entered—or was shoved into—a dreamy state. No doubt I was doped up on a testosterone overdose. As sometimes happens in a dream, things suddenly seemed to lack meaning or menace. I was surprised that my father's bulletproof jacket now fit just fine. Perhaps the mermaids had altered it. Perhaps they had altered me.

The auburn handed me my grandfather's sword, and she helped my affix it to a baldric. She seemed so pretty as she knelt and handed to me the blade. It was a solemn and cere-monial gesture, and suddenly, I was sorry that Penny was not there to see it. In the next moment, I was angry that all these sisters and cousins of Penny were not her. I was angry at myself for being so attracted to any other woman. What kind of man did that make me? Not a hero, certainly.

I tried to use my tone of voice to warn them back. "Brave! Clean! Cleaner than this, any way. Reverent. God help me."

That brought a moment of clarity to my thoughts. I shrugged my shoulders and tossed the women away from me. To my surprise, they did not fall on their well-shaped fannies, but merely floated back, hanging in the air, their hair as weightless clouds around them.

Air? I looked around. We had left the sleeping chamber. I was standing on a tongue like a dock protruding into a covered canal or tube. It looked like a waterslide at a theme park. Behind me was the curving wall of the bubble-shaped chamber I had just left. Through the glassy surface, I could see the teenaged girls I had saved from Ur, still sleeping. I was underwater once more, but it was not choking me. I wondered if this were some sort of hyper-oxygenated fluid or a magic spell meant to allow land-dwellers to survive the outdoors.

I was surrounded by the all-girl band. The honey-blonde made an imperious gesture. One redhead tucked her fiddle beneath her chin and began to bow. The other banged her tambourine against her shapely palm and shapely hip. One brunette put her lips to the twin flutes, and the shrill melody and harmony entwined each other. The other strummed sultry arpeggios on the lute, weaving theme within theme.

The sound actually carried better underwater. But I suppose it must have been magic water or something since you would think wetting the strings would ruin them, if they are anything like bowstrings.

The music began pulsing inside my bloodstream and brain again.

I said, "Oh, no, you don't!" and I shouted out a blasphemy. At least, when I started to say it, I meant it as a blasphemy, but once the name left my lips, I felt it was like a prayer, and so I added, "Have mercy on us!"

The music lost some of its hold on me. My fingers unthinkingly closed on the hilt of Dancing Maiden. Now what? Perhaps I could slap the girls around or break their instruments to halt the music, but that did not seem very much in keeping with the twelve points of the Scout Law I had just been reciting.

I reached up and yanked my ears off. Yes, I tore the delicate flesh of my ears directly out of my skull, and two clouds of blood began spreading over my shoulders. They screamed, and I bellowed, and I am pretty sure they stopped playing their song. But at that point, I did not care because it really, really hurt.

They were duly freaked out. In fact, the redhead, the auburn, and one brunette left their instruments floating where they were dropped, turned tail, and swam away. It was supernaturally quick, supernaturally graceful flight. Each put her arms behind her and kicked both legs together so that the whole body formed on continuous eel-like sinewave. It looked more as if the waters gathered around them and carried them away in a current.

The lutist held her ground, and so did the honey-blonde with the mirrored spellbook. I clutched my ear tatters to either side of my aching skull, concentrated, and willed my head together. Then, I straightened up and called my blood back into me. The cloud rushed into my mouth and nostrils in three red streams. The lutist fled at that point.

I straightened up. There was the honey-blonde hanging in the water above me, as beautiful as a fashion model, her skin glowing with inner light. I pointed at my ear and then at the lonely violin still spinning in the current. "Hey! No more of that! Capice? Otherwise, me heap big mad. You grok?" I waved my finger at her. "*La-la-la* bad! Bad mermaid! Bad! No *la-la-la*."

She inclined her head in a regal nod. "*No-la la-illa.*"

At that moment a carriage or coracle shaped like a clam shell being pulled by dolphins in harness like a foursome of horses came down the tunnel of air to the landing were we stood and docked.

A sea maid with a coronet and a choker of abalone shells and carrying a whip sat in the bow, holding the gossamer strands that served as reins. Two more maidens with pale blonde hair clung gracefully to the stern. They wore a tighter and darker arrangement of translucent bands; these garments were slightly more modest, more like one-piece swimsuits, and had no trailing tails. I wondered if this were some sort of uniform. I saw that the coracle passed across the coating of the bottom of the tunnel. This coating parted with less resistance than water, without turbulence or spray, as frictionless as oil.

The honey-blonde said something in Circassian and gestured toward the coracle with a graceful inclination of her head.

It seemed I was to be taken somewhere.

"So nice of you to ask so nicely," I said to the honey-blonde. "Better than being drugged and led about like a bull with a ring in his nose. I am a little worried about my gaggle of rescued co-eds back there. I promised I would get them home. Nothing bad better happen to them!"

"*No-la la-illa,*" she said agreeably, beckoning.

I tentatively put my hand to the curved surface of the tube of air. It stretched under my fingers. The honey-blonde touched me gently on the shoulder, and she kicked herself through the surface and drew me with her.

It was like walking through a curtain of beads if the beads were softly trying to pet and caress as you pushed through them. Like everything else that brushed against my skin in this place, it sent ripples of pleasure through me.

As the substance passed over, it kept all the water with it. The substance in my lungs was turned to air instantly, gently and with no more disturbance than a burp. It left a refreshing mint taste in my throat and cleared my sinuses.

"Best airlock ever!" I said to the honey-blonde.

"*No-la la-illa,*" she said nodding, beckoning me into the coracle.

The coracle turned out to be a big clamshell, curved like a shallow bowl. There was no flat and even place to sit. There were soft silk pillows gathered in the vessel's belly to recline upon. These pillows, and everything else, including me, tended to slip toward the center.

Scattered among the pillows were warm translucent bubbles of wine and spiced wine, as well as smaller bubbles of hot oil for combing into one's hair. Somehow these bubbles did not pop when you sat on them. I could not get them to pop at all. But the honey-blonde could twist the wine bubbles with her sharp, rose-red fingernails to form a pucker or nipple to suckle at, which was frankly a little weird.

She also insisted on brushing and combing my hair during the ride. I am not sure what was in the hair oil, but for the first time my wire scrub-brush hair looked all shiny and lustrous. I liked it, but I was not sure if I was supposed to like it. It was too much like a girl's hair.

And there was no way to sit upright in the smooth curving belly of the shell. The only way to sit was to lay yourself down on the pillows, and there was no place to go if the two showgirls following climbed in over the stern to help the honey-blonde pour hot wine in your mouth and comb your yards of hair while they chattered and giggled in a language you cannot speak. You had to kind of snuggle up because the swaying of the carriage kept pushing you together.

I liked it, but I was not sure if I was supposed to like it. I was pretty sure I was not.

We passed through a tunnel made of air that curved through a midair lake where fish and maidens sported.

We passed above and below wonders of beauty, aquariums and gardens, and came to a large central sphere where dozens of airy tubes and canals gathered. I saw many gardens, neatly trimmed, but only one arbor. It was huge and hanging just above the large central bubble. Don't think of a greenhouse; think of a dome ten times the radius of the Houston Astrodome, holding a hundred acres of old growth pine, oak, ash, and elm. Hills were piled near the middle. A little river curved through the wood, came to the edge of the circle, and fell out of the curved walls as a waterfall.

We passed into something like a cavern of air beneath a curving roof of glass and through a lagoon filled with coracles like ours. Lightly, the vessel came to the edge of a landing or quay. The quay was made of a soft and yielding carpet of blue-green fibers that embraced the coracle's rim without jarring or bumping it. A ramp of pink lead from the quay to a circular valve like a clamshell set in the sloping wall of opaque glass looming above.

On the quay stood a young man of stalwart build. He was erect of spine and broad of shoulder. He wore a jetpack on his back, a white motorcycle jacket, white pants, and black boots. Slung at one hip was a pistol with a strange triangular barrel I recognized from pictures in science magazines as a miniature version of a rail gun. It was a silent magnetic caterpillar gun, like those being experimentally used on warships, but hand sized. To his other side, he wore a Heckler & Koch submachine gun in a thigh holster.

He turned. The man was wearing a bone-white motorcycle helmet with a mirrored visor. The jacket had articulate metal plates at the chest and shoulders reaching to his groin, like police riot gear. The helmet had antennae, giving him a definite spaceman vibe. The guy must have been on the phone because he touched his glove to his ear, and the antenna retracted. In his pallid armor, he would have looked too much like a stormtrooper from *Star Wars* except there was a ruby-red cross filling the front panel of his jacket. He was a crusader.

As he turned, I saw a blade I recognized sheathed at his harness. I stared at it, puzzled. It had the distinctive S-shaped crosspiece and the lion-head pommel of a Swiss Guard dress sword. I had seen it hanging on the wall in my house.

The mirrored faceplate turned down to inspect me. I could see my distorted reflection, very tiny, and the pink, bright bodies curving next to me.

I was lying in the bottom of the cushioned with a half-naked woman snuggled up to either side of me, holding bubbles of wine to my mouth for me to suckle on, with heaps of hair being combed and primped by a third.

The mirrored visor of the helmet slid upward, revealing his face.

"Ilya? Is that you? What the hell are you doing here?"

It was Alexei. My older brother.

6

POOR FELLOW-SOLDIER OF THE TEMPLE OF SOLOMON

1. Brother Mine

*A*lexei's stern expression, gold eyebrows, bronze tan, and steel-blue eyes made his face a metal mask. His chiseled, narrow features bore a tougher, leaner look than when last I had seen him so long ago. It seemed a lifetime. Was it actually less than a year?

He was not as high minded and smoothed tongued as our middle brother, Dobrin. Alexei was fond of practical jokes, and he knew how to hold a grudge. But I saw no devilish, fun-loving twinkle in his eye now. He was changed.

I rocked the coracle in my eagerness to leap out and nearly capsized it. I made a pratfall in the process, but I leaped to my feet again with a gush of giddy laughter. I felt so buoyant that I was not sure whether I was in air or water.

I threw up my arms to embrace him, but instead of returning my smile, he fended me off with an upraised hand. As suddenly as a record scratch interrupting the bouncy and happy theme that is supposed to play when long lost brothers meet, I was deflated.

"It's me!" I protested.

"What's with the hair?" He scowled.

"It grew."

"You are six inches taller than you used to be." His scowl deepened.

"I grew. Or maybe it is the Oobleck."

"The which-what?"

"Oobleck. My name for the goo Uncreation is made of. It reacts to thought. You see, I am actually from a demon world called Cainem, and... well, I am not your brother."

"Powers... demon world... so you admit you are *not* Ilya?" His face darkened. "Why are you impersonating his form, creature?"

"Have you gone crazy? It's me!"

He said, "My brother died!"

"Listen! I can prove it! Ask me something only I would know!"

"Mm. What did I score in the regionals last season?"

"What? I don't care about your dumb games. The only reason I went when we were younger is that. Mom made me go!"

"The real Ilya loved going to games!"

"For the cheerleaders! I never looked at the field."

"You are not him!"

"Wait!" My voice got louder as my frustration grew. "I can prove it. Do you remember the time you blamed me for spilling the chocolate raisins on Christmas morning, and you pounded on me all the way from the kitchen to the dining room to the den and back again? Well, it was Dobrin who spilled them!"

"What are you talking about?" he shouted back. "I don't remember that! That never happened!"

"How could you not remember?!" My bellow drowned

his. "You beat the snot out of me on Christmas Day! It was the worst day of my life!"

"Wait a minute. You mean the year you knocked down the Christmas tree and ruined everything for everyone?"

"Me? I did not knock down the *chyortov* Christmas tree, you *chyort* liar! You shoved me into it!" (I used an impolite Russian word, glad that Abby was not around to hear it.)

He shouted back. "*Chush' sobach'ya!*" (The phrase was more impolite than mine. It referred to bull manure.) "You lie about everything! You want people to feel sorry for you, don't you? You live off sympathy like a vampire lives on blood! Well, Mom used to go to bed crying because of you! I could hear her through the wall!"

By this time, my blood was hot, and the hairs hanging down my back started to lift up weightlessly, swaying and snapping in the angry wind, but, of course, there was no wind. I could feel the blood pulsing in my face, a warm blush of anger. The Pobleck in my blood surged and stormed as anger tingled in the air between us.

He shouted, "The only crybaby in the house was you! I never cried!"

I shouted, "Because you are self-centered, cold-hearted fish, Alexei!" Except instead of *fish*, I used a word referring to the male member.

From the look on his face, I realized I must look something awful: blazing eyes and face black with wrath. Yards of hair swaying like the snakes of medusa probably did not help convince him I was human. Which, come to think of it, I was not. Not really. His grim expression grew grimmer.

"You are not him." He raised a pistol in one fist and a crucifix in the other.

2. Prayer to Benedict

The half-naked showgirls, seeing this, cooed and giggled ominously. Don't ask me how to giggle ominously. I don't know how. But they did.

Swaying and smiling, eyes bright beneath half-closed lids, the sea maidens surrounded us. The warm perfume from their long and shining hair was in the air. The girls reached out with soft hands and with youthful, rounded, naked arms, urging us apart, gesturing for Alexei to put the crucifix down. Either they did not know what a pistol was or did not fear it.

One started reciting a soft, murmuring, lyrical chant, dripping and syrupy with somnolent, soporific notes. The others joined in until all were singing. The song made my anger fade, and the soft, warm notes soothed away whatever thoughts I was trying concentrate on. The comfortable, sinuous, relaxing feeling wrapped my limbs and relaxed the swaying snake-nest of my hairdo. My yard-long bangs submitted to the law of gravity once more.

Alexei shook aside the attempted embraces. He flourished the cross. His voice was stern and harsh. "In the name of the Father, the Son, and the Holy Ghost, get thee back, bedamned witches!"

My head cleared a little. I took out Father's ivory crucifix that held the finger bone of Saint Demetrius of Sermium in a small glass reliquary. The reliquary was yellow with the oil the bone exuded.

I held it up toward the face of the girl trying to wind her hands around my bicep. "*O glorious St. Benedict, sublime model of all virtues, pure vessel of God's grace!*"

Alexei waved his cross up and down, side to side, and repeated the gesture twice more, starting with his left. The girls on that side of him took a step back and then two. He said, "*Behold me, humbly kneeling at thy feet. I implore thy loving heart to pray for me before the throne of God.*"

I flourished my cross to my right. The red-lipped, raven-haired beauty to my right gave me a smile as she stepped back, but the smile suddenly seemed fake and forced, like something a bored model hired to sell toothpaste might wear. *"To thee I have recourse in all the dangers which daily surround me."*

"Shield me against my enemies. Inspire me to imitate thee in all things." He turned and gestured behind him. The girls behind him dropped silver pan-pipe and double-flute clattering to the dock, startled.

I also turned and displayed my cross to a lovely lutist sneaking up on me, strumming her strings. "May thy blessing be with me always so that I may shun whatever God forbids and avoid the occasions of sin." She held up her lute of golden wood before her eyes, shielding them while she inched backward.

"Amen," said we as one.

The singing seemed suddenly flat and strange, as if it were now merely modulated air vibrations, not a living chant. The choir diminished into an awkward mumble. One enthused siren, a young blue-eyed redhead, diligently carried on for a few more bars before her voice trailed off into miserable silence.

Alexei looked me in the eye. "Benedict, eh?"

I said, "I thought it appropriate, considering." Benedict of Nursia was the patron saint against witchcraft, poisoning, and temptations of the flesh.

"So you really are you," said Alexei. He holstered his pistol. "But what are you? In God's name, how are you alive? How can you possibly be alive?"

I looked left and right at the circle of unearthly beauty queens. They all stood in the relaxed, practiced posture of fashion models, smiling, one leg slightly forward, hips cocked, shoulders back. I said casually, "You think these mermaids are recording everything we are saying? I know Penny speaks English."

"I know that we bug them when they visit our soil. Who is Penny?"

"The daughter of the boss. My boss."

"Who?"

"You know the Cryptozoology Museum where I work. Worked. Professor Dreadful's daughter? Sailed around the world solo?"

"You are always mooning over some girl. I thought you were sweet on Twig Schmidle."

"There is a gorgeous, world-famous girl with the outrageously unlikely name of Penny Dreadful who moved into our dumb little hometown, and you don't remember her? She is a—" I stopped, the words stuck in my throat.

3. A True Knight's Son

The realization dazed me. I was the baby seal, and the sudden truth I saw was the club.

"—Dad must have known." My voice was harsh. "When I showed him the message from Professor Dreadful about the Moebius gate in the basement of the Haunted Museum leading to other worlds, he did not turn a hair. Dad had been watching the professor, or been warned about him, or something. How could he not know Penny was a spy from another dimension? Then why did he let me work at the cryptozoology museum without saying a word?"

I looked at my so-called brother in sudden suspicion, at his eyes as blue as the winter skies of Kiev, his hair as yellow as wheat from the Ukraine. A human face from Albion. Not the aeon I came from.

I said slowly, "You are a Templar. You must know all this, too. Since when? Ever since you came back from Italy, right?

That is when you started getting all weird. So you knew, too."

His face grew stiff and his eyes cold. "If by *weird*, you mean *grown up*, yes. Not everyone in the family can afford to be mollycoddled and protected from the truth..."

"You knew!"

"Knew what? That you were some freak? Sure. I assume everyone in town knew. Just by looking at you. Caveman manners and apeman face, Ilyusha. Holy *hooey* of Christ! The hours I spent trying to convince my friends that you were all right, just one of the boys, just like everyone else... then you would go spend nights out in the woods like some sort of wild animal..."

"What? I am a Boy Scout! It is called camping!"

"When you were little, you killed a squirrel with your teeth and ate it raw. Mom had to go out looking for you."

"I don't remember that."

"See? You just conveniently forget when someone does something for you! Sometimes I could just kill you!" Suddenly, and for no reason, there were tears in his eyes, and suddenly, for no reason, in mine, and we were hugging each other fiercely. He pounded me on the back, and I pounded him on the rocket tubes of his jetpack.

Then, I shoved him away. "Everything in my life is lie! And you lied as much as Dad if you knew and didn't tell me!"

"That you were adopted? But you knew that also! And you know that does not matter. Mom loved you anyway. May she rest in peace. And the rest of us almost tolerated you." He crossed himself.

I stood dumbfounded. "Dad didn't tell you? Does he lie to everyone? Not just me? I guess I should feel good about that."

"Lie about what? What are you talking about?"

"She's alive! Mom is alive!"

He face looked like a deflated balloon. "What? The hell you say."

"Alive! Alive! She is in a place called Sabtechah in a buried city called Agarththa, hidden in their version of Tibet, beneath Lhasa. Dad gave me a letter."

"Letter? Let me see it."

"Lost it. Sorry."

"What? Where?"

"I dropped it off the edge of the Dark Tower when the moon got eaten. That was before I was mugged by a nudist vampire, fell to my death, and got captured by the crew of steampunk Babylonians. Then, there were a few months of being tortured in a spiky birdcage, and I lost track of time. Sorry about losing a stupid letter that only has in it things Dad should have told us all when we were kids. Did he have a false funeral for me, too? Is it a family tradition?"

Alexei stepped back from me. His cheeks were still wet, but his eyes were like bright blue chips of ice. His voice was just as cold. "There were so many deaths the day you vanished, and no one has been able to recover all the bodies or estimate their number. These days, we just hold memorials for everyone lost or missing every week. You think you were ill used? Dad could not tell anyone the military secrets of our order. Neither can I. Can't tell you that you are from a parallel dimension because the existence of parallel dimensions is a secret we have to keep from everyone. And for a damned good reason, too!"

"What's the reason?"

"Can't tell you that…"

My temper broke free like a wild stallion breaking its hawser. I doubled up my fist and drew back, ready to break some of the perfect teeth in his sneering, supercilious, big-brotherly face.

But my brother was still talking "...after all, we were trying to prevent disasters like what you caused."

That splashed cold water on my soul. My fist trembled, as my arm suddenly lacked strength. "Who caused? Not me! What are you talking about?"

"Millions of people on Earth are dead because someone broke the rules of the Arcanum. You. The Dark Tower broke into our world because of you. Dad took the blame, and now he is going to be killed. Because of you." And he punctuated the sentence with another Russian swearword, one of the more vile ones.

Killed?

I was standing there with my mouth hanging open, dead inside, when an amber-eyed redhead kissed me lightly on the ear and whispered something in a language I did not know.

She pointed.

4. Psamathe

All the other girls, as pretty as flowers whom a gentle wind makes lower their heads, had touched knee to carpet. The ones dressed in filmy scarves curtseyed while the ones dressed in tighter, darker sheaths of material knelt. If these the outfits denoted rank, the higher-ups were draped in longer and brighter scarves than the underlings.

Even Alexei—I saw from the corner of my eye—made a snappy military salute, forearm parallel to the ground, elbow and fingers one straight line, fingertips touching his visor bright above the right eye.

The girl next to me touched my shoulder, silently urging me to bow. I ignored her, instead but turned and raised my eyes to see who it was.

"Penny!" I called out, relieved and astonished.

At the top of the ramp leading up from the quay, framed

in a circular valve opening into the curving glass wall above us, there she stood, poised like a glamour model.

It was Penny. It was she!

Her demeanor was entirely changed; she held herself with the dignity of a queen. I almost did not recognize her. She was more beautiful than before, her gold hair shining more brightly, her lips redder and fuller, her emerald eyes more regal.

Her figure was more voluptuous than yesterday, her curves more rounded, her waist trimmer, her hips more exquisite, and legs longer and more shapely. She was dolled up: Ornaments of pearl and mother-of-pearl adorned her brow, ears, throat, wrists, waist, and ankles. The scarf-tails trailing from shoulder and hip were held by a row of blonde maidens demurely waiting on her. If length of tassel did indeed indicate ranks in mermaid land, Penny was yards above all others here.

In one hand, she held a luminous wand. She gestured with it. A little dot of light from the wand flickered on the ground at my feet and then danced up the slope, as if beckoning me to follow.

I loped up the ramp, grinning in relief. I flung out my arms, readying a boisterous bear-hug. "Penny! I wondered where you got to..."

Alexei hissed, "Ilyusha!"

The sharp note in his voice was like a splash of cold water. Only then, I saw the looks of shock, amusement, and horror on the faces of the maidens clustered on the ramp. All were staring at me. Some displayed impish curiosity, smothering smiles, and some were aghast, eyes wide.

The cold knife of embarrassed shame slid into my heart. Something was wrong.

I looked again at Penny. Her hair was more golden, and her figure more curvaceous, her leg longer, precisely because this was not Penny. A sister, almost a twin; but not Penny. The look in her eye was too majestic, too cold.

To her, I was no one. She was looking at a stranger.

I lowered my arms and cleared my throat.

Alexei marched up the ramp double time, his arms and armor clanging at his footfall. He saluted the lady again and said something in a language I did not know, "*Psh`eshuxe pshashe dexeded! K'yshujeg'jeg'u…*"

She interrupted him and spoke in a voice like a golden harp, ringing. She was not chanting an enchantment, but the natural lilt of her voice, even when speaking prose, was poetic. Even when curt, it smote the ear with beauty.

She pointed the wand at him, then at me, and uttered a command.

Alexei nodded politely to her and turned to me. He spoke without moving his lips in a tense voice. "What have you messed up now, Ilyusha? Why is the princess asking for you?"

I said, "I escaped from the Dark Tower, rescued one hundred fifty-one girls from a fate worse than death, and helped one of these sea witches complete her mission. If you speak this language, I have some questions. Where is Parthenope?" I turned toward the regal young woman that looked so much luck her and said the name loudly and clearly. "Parthenope…?"

She said to me, "*Si-ts'e Psamathe Xägwacha. Parthenope shäpkhu si.*"

Alexei said, "She says she is Sandy the sea-princess. Maidensong is her sister."

She then said in her sharp but lovely voice, "*Shuqek'osht!*" I did not need a translation for that. *Follow!*

With this, she turned on her heel, and her maidens wheeled with her and swayed after her, graceful as ballerinas, sensuous as she-panthers, as she departed into the interior of the great glass pearl.

Alexei stepped forward, and I did, too. He put out a hand to bar my way. "Where do you think you are going?"

I said, " Where do you think *you* are going? I was brought here by my all-girl band behind us there and obviously not to talk to you. I am not sure whether I am a guest or a patient or a prisoner, frankly. This place gives me the creeps. The girls are way too friendly…"

"…Too friendly for someone who looks like Bobo the Ape-Boy, you mean."

I gave him a brotherly smack on the head, but my knuckles just bounced off his helmet. He turned and brought up his forearm to block, but he was too slow for me; he drove his fingers, knife-hand style into my sternum, and I was too slow for him. I doubled over, gasping.

The ladies behind gasped or tittered, and the ones ahead turned graciously, arching graceful eyebrows above pretty and glittering eyes. Roughhousing was evidently an odd sight to see in the floating city under the sea.

Alexei nonchalantly hooked a foot around my ankle and shoved me to my knees while I was bent double with coughing. "Act your age," he said. "I am here with the diplomatic entourage from the Holy Father. Any little thing might mess up the talks. Or, in your case, any big, hairy, stupid thing. The Apostolic Legate is being housed in that red dome over there. That is the embassy."

He pointed to a pink bubble that hovered next to a larger bubble housing the vast indoor forest I had noted before. If the important bubbles were docked near the center of the city, the embassy dome was one of the most important.

He said, "Get lost and go there until my duty here is over. That big canal runs toward it. Tell the Grandmaster I sent you. We'll talk. You have a lot to answer for."

It did not seem fair that a blow to the solar plexus could mess me up more than a spear through the heart. Even

JOHN C. WRIGHT

though I was an Undying of Cainem, he had found a way to throw me. Must be big-brotherly instinct.

I glared up at him. "Your days of pounding on me are over, Alyosha. I am a monster now."

He said, "I am a knight of the Templars now. We slay monsters."

He gave me that same cocky, crooked smile as on the Christmas morning, so many years ago, when he threw me into the Christmas tree and got everyone to blame me for it. A day he said he had forgotten.

I had not had the power, not then, to wipe it off his smug face. But now?

Now, I could feel the fiery strength of the shadow-substance in my immortal veins and muscles swelling as my anger swelled. The muscles in my arms and chest expanded. As I rose to my feet, I had to unzip my father's flack jacket, afraid the seams might burst if I did not.

"Whoa, whoa!" he said, backing up. His voice was sharp, but his eyes were cold and unwinking. "I just told you there is serious business afoot."

"Breaking your jaw will be serious. Maybe then you would shut up for once and listen to what I told you." I watched his hands, grinning my biggest, square-toothed gargoyle grin, waiting for him to draw some weapon that could not possibly kill me, waiting for an excuse to pluck it out of his hands and stuff it up his nose.

He surprised me and moved not a finger. Instead, he said, "Okay. I'm listening."

Without turning her head or slowing her pace, Psamathe called out one ringing word. "*Shuqek'osht!*"

Alexei had no choice. He started walking again. I fell in step alongside, aching to punch him in his face. With a rustle of silks and a whispering murmur of soft voices, the girls behind us followed.

He said. "I am listening, but I only have until we enter the presence chamber. How are you alive? What are you doing here?"

I said, "I am alive because I am a monster from some world where Dad found me as a baby. I can rip off my own head and not die. You've heard of an aeon called Cainem?"

"Yes. You cannot be one of them. When we were young, I saw you get bloody noses and stuff... I mean..."

"Gave me a bloody nose, you mean. But how often did you see me in fatal accidents? Never. Until you are killed, being unkillable just does not come up. Not until I fell into a Moebius gate. There was nothing on the other side. Literally. A storm of swirling, burning, sticky, floaty, solid nothing. Some of it is inside my body and is still there."

"A working gate?"

"Dad did not tell you that, either, huh? Professor Dreadful and his daughter are agents of the Wisecraft. I am here because I escaped from the Dark Tower to this world, and these mermaids brought me here. I had friends with me, but I don't know what they did with them. I swore to get everyone home, and I will."

"Mermaids?" He snorted.

"What do you call them?"

"*Maleficae Maris*. Their word for themselves is *Psämwädä*."

"So why are you here?"

He said, "Their princess asked the Legate if I could translate. There is a prisoner they want to question who speaks Latin."

I said in Latin, "More skillfully, I speak the tongue of the English."

His eyes widened. "You?"

"Looks like," I grunted. "I had been really hoping I was an honored guest."

"What did you do this time, Ilyusha?"

Of course it was my fault. It was always my fault. "I got adopted into the wrong family. As I child, I was fed a straight diet of deception." I wanted it to come out in a joking tone, but instead the words were bitter.

Alexei surprised me again. "*Ne volnujsja!*" ("Not to worry!") He said softly, "Now that you are alive, I am never going to let them lock you up. Not these witches. Not anyone. Your big brother is here to keep you out of trouble. Again."

I was not sure how to take that. Was he actually on my side for once? I gave him a skeptical look. "Never? Or not until your diplomatic mission gets in the way, you mean."

He said " I mean *never*! While this stalwart knight and true of the Temple of Solomon has blood in his veins, sword in his hand, and God in his heart, no one puts my brother in chains. So swear I."

5. The Presence Chamber

We entered a curving, barrel-vaulted corridor paved in nacre. The sloping walls looked like they had been grown from the inside of a nautilus shell, not built of bricks.

Round pools of water we had to circle were set in the floor and also in the walls and ceiling like wide, round windows and skylights. You could stick you hand through the surface, and little tremors of pleasure would run up and down your arm. Yanking your hand back would not splash any water in, but would clean bloody knuckles since the boundary allowed solids to pass through freely, but no liquid. Beyond these round windows were winding horizontal corridors and curving vertical shafts filled with water. Fair-haired bathing beauties darted as gracefully a goldfish up and down their sinuous lengths.

In one quarter, the pools grew larger, met, and merged so

that soon the procession trod a narrow catwalk or set of stepping stones through a solid but unwalled corridor of air.

The tube we trod spiraled inward toward the center of the bubble-shaped palace, meaning we made a complete circle of the place, or more than one, as we approached the central chamber.

The central chamber was a sphere wider than the eye could see. The light came from a crowd of bubbles gathered near the center. All else was dusk and dim.

The upper part was water, and killer sharks of motley black and white circled and swam unceasingly, and squids larger than any seen on our world coiled writhing arms, their miters and mantles gleaming with colors.

Lights played along this rippling ceiling above us. It was claustrophobic to walk under countless metric tons of rippling water being held nonchalantly aloft by nothing.

I had been wondering why no Beefeaters or Praetorian guards were around, like you see in throne rooms in the movies; now I was wondering whether the mermaids could simply drop the ceiling at the snap of a finger and crush or drown any air-breathers caught beneath.

Meanwhile, underfoot, the lower part of the spherical chamber was liquid. It was separated from us by a substance as clear as ice but warm to the touch.

It was, however, slippery. Psamathe and her maidens slid forward as gracefully as ice skaters. Each flung back her arms and raised her rear leg in arabesque, circling and pirouetting. If you've ever seen dignitaries like the Queen of England at a coronation or a royal wedding moving with stiff solemnity, this looked nothing like that. It was more like seeing the dignity of swans swimming or cats grooming.

Meanwhile, Alexei and I were taking little baby steps on the slippery surface. Bathing beauties darting and playing underfoot, half hidden in the clouds of their own hair, peered up at us, goggling and giggling.

Strawberry blondes and light-brown brunettes dressed in clinging wisps, smiling, slid up behind the two of us, putting soft hands on our elbows and shoulders, offering to escort our clumsy selves across the ice.

Alexei shooed the women away from him, bent his knees, and jumped. Wings from his backpack snapped open, and a high-pitched roar issued from jet turbines at the wing tips.

He only fired a burst or two when he was high up in the air, so no one underfoot was caught in the downwash. For the second half of his arc of flight, he did not fall. Instead, brass-colored cylinders or capsules fixed to strategic points on his harness and armor glowed with an eerie blue-white radiation and slowed his fall. He floated downward like a paratrooper and landed with his knees bent.

The jetpack I recognized as technology from my world; perhaps the antigravity electromagnets—or whatever they were—were a technomancy from some allied aeon.

It was still cool as all get-out, and yes, maybe I was a little jealous. After all, Alexei had been allowed to drive the family jeep three years before I was. Now this.

My only retaliation was to put my arms tightly around the trim waists of the warm, hourglass-shaped beauties helping me walk across the ice. Both snuggled close, smiling, and put a soft cheek against either bicep.

Meanwhile, Psamathe seated herself on the lower valve of a great clamshell. The winding shape of a sea-serpent, which I thought was a jade statue until it blinked, curled behind her. Its throat was her backrest. The cobra-hood of the monster was a canopy above her head. She draped her white arms across loops of its sinuous body to her left and right.

Before the throne were courtiers, all female, young, blonde, and pretty, with pearls in their hair, jewels in their navel, and bangles and bracelets at every joint. The filmy scarves falling from bows or corsages adorning décolletage or trailing from derriere of their lingerie-sheer bathing suits were held in the hands of brunettes dressed in tighter, darker bathing suits.

Girls dressed in gossamer scarves stood in a semicircle behind the throne, holding luminous wands. From their tips, every few minutes, an orb would swell, break free, and float upward, shining. This was the source of the glowing bubbles. They were gathered in a cloud above the throne like a swarm of lazy, overfed fireflies. From them came that fresh-scrubbed, tingling scent you sometimes smell on the wind after an electrical storm.

Alexei had scattered this cloud of glowing bubbles as he fell down to land in a polite kneeling posture before the throne so that, for a moment, it was dark around him. Alexei was a shadow as he rose to his feet, and the red cross on his chest was black and stark against his ghostly white armor.

One person was not standing. Kneeling next to the throne was a brunette in a beehive hairdo, who had an open book resting across her knees. Perhaps she was a court reporter. The pages were stiff, thin sheets of gold alloy. The brunette had an instrument in hand which could have been a stylus or a sewing needle. The shorthand was written in waxy, colored threads woven like macramé running between small holes punched in the metal. Her fingers flew nimbly, invisibly swift, as the conversation ran. There was no ink to run or paper to sag if the document were accidentally submerged.

Psamathe spoke in a halting Latin. Her grammar about as bad as mine.

"Servant of Cardinal Abibo Shukeshiko, who serves the Holy Father Peter the Second in the Golden City, who serves the Anointed Child of Heaven, whom we do not name; from the lips of the Sea-queen, Iaera, daughter of Maera, she sends her greetings and blessings, and her bound word of safe conduct: to and from this place the Servant of the Anointed Child may pass without let or hindrance. Her daughter, Psamathe serves her, and she serves the Wise of the Nine Worlds, who serve the beauty, terror, and glory of Nature and the ten thousand goddesses of Nature. In the name of your masters, I ask you to carry my words to this one." She tilted her wand at me. "He is our beloved guest, but curiosity, always the weakness of women, whirls our heads like wine, and we wish him to slake our hot thirst. Of all sensations, dryness of lip and throat is that in which the daughters of the sea delight in least."

Alexei turned to me and muttered. "What is going on?"

I dropped my voice, "She meant to say *gnatarum* in the genitive, not in the ablative. *Gnatis mari* means 'daughters out of the sea,' doesn't it?"

He said, "Stop being an idiot. Why are they asking me to translate a language you speak?"

I had been puzzling over that myself. If Parthenope or Foster had given a full report to their bosses among the Wisecraft, my name and origin would have been known. On the other hand, the mermaids here had seen me wound myself and regenerate, so they knew I was an abomination of aeon called Cainem, an immortal. A Cainem long in the service to the Dark Tower would have been familiar with Ursprache and understand all tongues, which I obviously did not. So who or what did they think I was?

I answered Alexei. "I cussed at them when I woke up and spoke the Name the witches do not say. They must have thought you could speak my lingo since we use the same name for the Savior. But it means the people I came with are either dead or not saying a word. That means something dangerous is here, right where everything should have been nice and safe."

He looked wary when I said this. "That means I should warn Dad and tell the Cardinal."

"Dad's here?" My head felt light with relief.

"With the Legate and emissaries from all our worlds."

"What is he doing here?"

"This is the Council of Elrond."

"Really? I thought this was Castle Anthrax from Monty Python."

"No, from Tolkien. You remember—"

"I remember. The Templars are meeting with the Wisecraft?"

He gave me a narrow eyed look. "You know about that, do you?"

"What is the council for?"

"Alliance. It is kind of tense because each side burned the other side at the stake or threw them to lions in our different versions of history. So you popping up here, this particular random spot where the floating capital city of their whole confederation randomly happens to be floating on by is really unrandom-looking to them. And to me. So everyone is on edge."

"Why?"

"We have found something like the One Ring, a super-weapon that might end the war."

I snapped my fingers. "Does this have anything to do with something called the Colossal Zoetic Panoply? And a Moses-looking man named Ossifrage?"

"His name is Jonah, but yeah. Him. How did you know about him?"

"I saved him. He's here, unless the mermaids took him elsewhere while I slept."

"Pretty sneaky."

"Mermaids are sneaky. At least three of the people from our hometown were spies keeping an eye on Dad. They must know his family. They know you. Why they don't know me, I don't know."

"Everyone thinks you are dead. You are taller. You look different."

I shook my head. A slight difference in appearance would not fool anyone for long. So it must all be pretense, play-acting. They were playing dumb hoping I'd spill something.

Psamathe cleared her throat and spoke in Circassian. Alexei listened carefully, and then he spoke in Latin to the brunette scribe in the beehive hairdo, who repeated and clarified what had just been said. The princess was politely asking whether I had been told her words yet and what my answer was.

I said to Alexei, "Tell the princess I will answer her questions."

He said back, "In other words, you are going to lie like a dog?"

I shook my head. "I cannot."

"No? Your favorite hobby, I thought. You turn over a new leaf or something?"

"Yes. Do you know how to stop a Dark Tower astrologer?"

"Astrologer?" He snorted. "That's funny... I mean, they summon up star-demons, so it sort of makes sense..."

"What do you call 'em?"

"*Praedivinator* or sometimes *Pythonicus*. The older term is *Chaldaean*."

"Same deal," I said dismissively. "Whatever they are, they have trouble seeing acts that spring from our higher nature. Evil deeds make our lives easier to predict. There is more too it, and I need help from Abby, a little girl who is my blood-brother, but I am tired of my sins helping my enemies. I am not going to lie."

"In practical terms, this is exactly the worst time to suddenly grow a conscience. Why don't you stick with what you are used to until the current crisis is past?"

I turned to princess Psamathe and bowed. "*Altissima domina*, I speak a little Latin. You may ask of me. I am true." Altissima meant "highmost." I hope it sounded polite.

Psamathe said, "You speak of small Latins? Or you are curt of speech? Short-tempered?" She kept a straight face, but she was teasing me.

Alexei addressed her in Latin. "He says he will answer with an honest tongue, if slow."

Psamathe raised a slender finger and spoke.

7

PRINCESS OF THE SUNLESS SEA

1. Quum Romae Fueris

I am going to leave out all of the hesitations and clarifications that followed. The dialog actually involved three or four people trying to translate, but I am giving it here as if everyone understood one another right off. It was frustrating. I had been missing Abby. Now I missed her patient willingness to use her gift of understanding.

The princess spoke:

"I am Psamathe, daughter of Iaera. In her name, the Covens of the Wise of the Sea greet and welcome you. We ask of you to name your name, and your fathers', and to say also in whose name you are come, a guest too impatient to await our invitation."

"I was born of an undying woman. She threw me aside when she wearied of me. What name she gave me, if any, I do not know. There is no marriage custom in that world, so I have no knowledge of what man mated with her."

This was the truth, but not the whole truth. I was sure

they knew who I was, but everything since I woke here had put me on edge. So I wanted to give away as little as possible.

I continued. "I do not come in anyone's name because I was brought. I was imprisoned by the Dark Tower of Ur, your enemies. Your sister, Parthenope, also a prisoner there, helped me escape, and this was the only place to go. She was with me. Where is she now? Please bring her here."

The princess said, "Other pleasures aside from speaking with her sister no doubt divert young Parthenope. Parthenope is well-loved here, and was thought lost, and so has many fond hands to clasp, joyful songs to sing, and kisses to bestow."

With these words, a certainty entered my heart that something had gone terribly wrong and that Penny was in a dungeon somewhere: Probably strapped to a gurney and getting electroshock therapy from monster electric eels. Or would mermaids bother? If songs could make you drunk or induce mesmeric trances, surely there was a siren song that acted like truth serum?

Psamathe said, "But curiosity still teases us. None depart the Dark Tower without their foreknowledge. If you are come here from them, it is either by their design or their permission."

That made me more unhappy. This sounded like Psamathe had not known why Parthenope had attempted to sneak into the Dark Tower. Which either meant that Penny had lied to me when she said she was a spy for the Wisecraft, or the Wisecraft were lying to me now and were pretending Penny was not one of their spies.

I suppose the third option was that her older sister Psamathe was not the spymaster who had originally sent Penny out on the mission and was not cleared to know.

In case that was so, I said, "I would like to speak to someone in authority."

Now the brunette kneeling next to the clamshell throne spoke up. "Wise Psamathe is here. Her word is a song in the heart of all who seek wisdom."

"Does that mean she leads the Wisecraft?"

That caused an almost-silent rustle of noise to pass through the chamber, as the gathered ladies in waiting exchanged glances, or sighed, or held their breath.

The brunette said, "Psamathe speaks for Iaera, who is the eldest of those whose art is the sea-wisdom!" Unlike Psamathe—and unlike me—her Latin grammar was flawless. Neither outlandish accent nor long hesitations blemished her speech.

Psamathe said gently, "The Wise of the Sea were once held in highest regard before we gathered to our hearts others covens of other aeons, wise-women, sibyls, and brides of the unseen. Those tides have ebbed. Now it is the Strega, the Wise in Dream-wisdom, who know greatest reverence. Yet even so, among the Wise, none shouts down others; none is too soft-spoken to go unheeded. All are sisters."

I said, "If the Wise who are older and wiser than wise Psamathe have kept back dark secrets, it would be wrong for me to uncover them."

Psamathe said, "It is not wrong to speak when beauty asks. Love holds naught back."

"The sisters of Parthenope well know she has a familiar called Wild Eyes. You know what can be hidden in the shadow of those wings if you are true sisters to Parthenope."

Psamathe raised an eyebrow at that. "You tie up your tongue? There is no need here."

"Noble lady, I am ignorant. But I do know that whatever your sister Parthenope has not said to you, I should not say. You said she's busy. When she is free, she can join us. She can tell you how we came out of the Dark Tower in a way their foresight did not foresee."

Psamathe smiled, and beauty, like a torch, began to glow in her eyes and to make her skin bright. She said, "All gathered here are of the coven of the Wise and well instructed in the mysteries. Am I not as fair as bright Parthenope?"

I just stared stupidly. "I am sure you are very pretty, Your Highness, but I wanted to speak to your sister to learn about, well, all about this place, and just what is going on here."

"This is Anthemoessa, the fairest queen of the flotilla cities. After the downfall of Panopeia on Everest Island to the Ur, the long-lived Cyrni died. Our widowed mothers brought their household goddesses here beneath the wave, and built and blessed Anthemoessa, and made her the capital of all the flotillas and tribes beneath the sea. Fear none here; we are creatures of love. Fate has wounded you cruelly; so we all observe! But ours is a house of wine and incense. Here neither spying sun nor jealous moon can reach any beam! No oath is asked."

"I still want to see her."

"You wish for the love-play with her? She is fair and buxom and sweetly callipygous."

"I—no, I did not say that—I wanted to—"

Psamathe looked impish. "You wish to *avoid* love-play with her? She disgusts you?"

A murmur of soprano disapproval rippled across the chamber. Girls chuckled or tittered, hissed or clucked.

Psamathe wagged a slim finger at me. "The hospitality of Anthemoessa cannot be thus impugned! Select of those gathered here or any you have seen from afar. You may have two or three or many, either at once or one after another. Oddities unlawful on your world are permitted here."

"No, thank you."

"I will comfort you myself if such is your secret desire. Speak your wish."

"No, thank you."

Psamathe said, "Is there not a saying on your world, *when in Rome, do as the Romans?*"

I was flustered. "Yes, ah, we have that saying."

She said, "We have a similar saying! It is our highest law. Do you scoff at our laws? Seem they backward or barbaric to you?"

Perhaps I should have been paying more attention to what she was saying. But I was sort of worried that all the cute girls here were seeing me blush. "No, Highness. I respect your way of life."

"Then what?" Again, she smiled impishly. "Are not all Eve's children kin? You think yourself our betters? We would obey your forms in your house. It was our rule of courtesy that bade us save the stranded traveler; yet you repay with scorn the rule that saved you!"

She was toying with me. I controlled my temper. "Highness, we also have rules. When a lower rule crosses a higher, the lower gives way. The rules of courtesy are high, but rules about love are highest. Our rule says there is no sex before the wedding and no adultery after."

The impish smile vanished. "How can this be if you are from an aeon where there is no marriage?"

I stood there with a dumb look on my face.

She said, "The ever-living abominations of Cainem neither keep oaths nor take them. Nor build they any cities, neither called Rome nor any other name, nor do they invent sayings. You have their abundance of life but have not their speech, nor their spirit, nor their ways."

All this time, all the lovely, silly girls in the chamber had been wearing charming smiles and stealing flirtatious glances at me. It was like a pleasant background music. Now the smiles ceased as suddenly as music going mute. Their eyes were cold and intent.

The silliness was just an act. The loveliness was just a weapon. These icy-eyed creatures were the real sirens.

Psamathe said, "Your tools are from an Incarnate World, the one we name Slaughter-of-Innocents, by the foe called Albion, and your sword is from the World of the Ten Thousand Spirits, called Amaterasu. About your neck is the crucifix of the Ecclesia, which is not found outside the worlds that branch off from Thoebel. A bright ghost protects you from our arts and guards your tongue and loins while you sleep. None of your hundred and fifty wives is so warded. Worship they different gods than yours?"

Alexei gave me a withering look. He did not have to say anything. When your brother has a look like that, you know what it means. *What stupid game are you playing, Ilyusha? If you lie, just lie. If you tell the truth, just tell it. If you are going to shut up, just shut up.*

Or maybe that was my conscience talking.

I straightened my spine. "My name is Ilya Vseslavyevich Bessmertniy Saint Mitrophan Muromets of the aeon called Albion. I worship the god who is both Son and Father, the god who is born as a man and was slain by man but who lives forever, whose name you are afraid to speak."

Now Psamathe leaned forward on her throne. "Man of Albion, we do indeed know of *Ule-Ne*, Crazy-Eye, the winged familiar of Parthenope, falcon-shaped. By this airy art, so strange to us, Parthenope hides from the omniscience of the Dark Tower. She alone of all sea-maidens learned the wood-sprite-craft of calling familiar spirits and the dream-craft of Cush. Despite her tender years, to her alone could be entrusted our gravest mission, on which all hope depends. Dashed hopes! We heard no word from her for a year, and the Dreaming Lady dreamed no dreams of her.

"Then, not long ago, we learned from a winged shadow that

our sister had been betrayed into the hands of the soldiery of the Darkest Tower and brought her living to await what is worse than death. Numbered among our allies are the warlock-lords of Riphath who study the dark elf lore. Theirs is a nocturnal cavalry of elfin steeds called the Night Riders. At the prayer of the Dreaming Lady of Cush, the submersible ironclad of Captain No One, Raja of the Sea, smuggled these cavaliers through seabed and twilight to Ur itself and breached the dreaded Euphrates River, whose waters fallen cherubim guard.

"All ended in ruin. The report reached our ears that the mission failed, all Nightriders slain but one, and him taken alive.

"And yet, behold, here you are, unscathed. Is this not cause for wonder?"

I was getting annoyed. "Parthenope is a witch. She broke me free of jail. I am an abomination of Cainem, who cannot die even if I want to, and no weapons stop me. I broke her out of jail. And as for your Night Riders, well, c'mon, some of them might just be jerks, who don't know when to trust their best friends. You know what I mean?"

Psamathe raised a slender hand. "Peace! Let no mistrust mar our sweet camaraderie! The sea is eager to embrace all. But surely these events must be known to us if our mutual love is to flourish. What do you know of Parthenope's capture? Tell your tale."

I said, "You are asking how she was captured? I know only what she told me."

The brunette said in flawless Latin, "A tale well-told grows more pleasing when spoken by other voices."

In other words, they wanted to compare my version with whatever Penny had told them and find discrepancies. So I said, "Sorry. The tale is hers to tell."

Psamathe spoke again. "It is your part in the tale we

fathom not. She cannot tell us this. Only you. How did you come into these events?"

Psamathe looked relaxed, but the other courtiers were as silent as images in a mirror, cold-eyed, motionless, waiting. Even the ladies under the floor, gliding in great circles, were making no startling moves.

Maybe I should have been more nervous. Maybe. But I really was not the enemy of these ladies. Was I?

I decided to stick to things they probably knew already or had guessed.

I said, "I was told she was in trouble. I went to save her."

"Wherefore?"

"To be a hero."

But my brother gave me a squinting look of disgust. Neither the princess nor her maidens snickered or scoffed or anything obvious like that.

Nor was it a lie. I thought it was true. I wanted it to be true.

But I saw how wrong my words rang. Everyone thought I was a dumb braggart.

Psamathe said, "Why send one so young into the Dark Tower?"

I laughed in relief. Small wonder the princess thought I was boasting!

It was an easy point to clear up. "Oh, no! No, ma'am! No one sent me to the Dark Tower. That is not what I meant!"

"Then where? Who sent you?"

"I was just going to the basement of the museum where I worked. My boss sent me. You see, he was studying the cuneiform letters left behind in the cloud chamber after the CERN supercollider disaster and trying to translate them. The cuneiform held the secret plans for how to build a Moebius coil. The Dark Tower sent a copy of the plans through the supercollider, hoping someone on our side would translate them and open a gate to let in their invasion force. So he built a model and powered it up and... uh..."

My voice trailed off. Alexei had a funny look on his face.

I suddenly saw what was wrong with the story.

Psamathe said, or sang, "Tell us his name. His name."

And the other sea maidens repeated the words in a choir, but oddly, as if they spoke syllables whose meaning they did not know. *Dic nomen ejus. Nomen ejus.*

Words came out of my mouth before I could bite my tongue. "Professor Dreadful. Achitophel Dreadful. His real name is Adramelech. He was pretending to be Parthenope's father, but he was actually one of your spies... and he lied to me about... everything..."

2. Nothing Said Makes Sense

I am not kidding about biting my tongue. I bit it in two and spat out the bloody tip and stood there scowling in pain. One squeamish mermaid fainted.

I was in a bad mood, and I prayed no prayers, so the regeneration took longer than normal. A minute, rather than seconds.

I just stood there, stock still, my eyes hot with unshed tears, and hot trickles of blood escaping from my clenched teeth and running down my chin.

Nothing in what I just said made sense.

For one thing, long before Professor Dreadful came to Earth, all the Wisecraft secret agents were surely aware of the methods and tactics of the Dark Tower. Adramelech certainly knew what a Moebius coil was and knew what would happen if he switched it on.

He surely knew how to read their cuneiform.

Second, why switch on the Moebius coil at all? In his note to me, he had pretended this was all new to him, a discovery of strange aeons beyond Earth. But he was actually a native of the strange aeons.

Third, what exactly had his mission been? To steal the secret plans? They were not secret. The enemy gave away blueprints to anyone in any world they could reach. Pally the plumber for the Dark Tower had told me their tactics. They hid nothing. Fate was fated.

Fourth, Adramelech's note to me said he had left the coil switched on and running, and I was supposed to switch it off; but when I arrived at the museum, it was just in time to see Penny switching on an entirely cold and safely switched-off apparatus.

Come to think of it: Why had she been doing that?

Okay, she had told me that Wild Eyes would prevent her deeds from being predicted by the bad guys, and she said the same thing about the ward she drew in the sea when she circumnavigated the globe. The gate activation should have been undetected. She did not think an invasion would enter my world.

But gates worked in pairs. Why turn on a receiver with no transmitter? Matching gates were meant to open into the same coordinates in Uncreation and dock like spaceship airlocks. Without a mate, no tube to another world would be formed. A one-sided gate would only open up into raw Uncreation. The only thing found there was Oobleck, which was a semi-solid form of twilight.

I remembered the blue light Penny had been burning from her broomstick. I had not recognized it then, but now I knew what it was: *ylemaramu*, the ghost-light to drive twilight away.

To do what? Not shut the gate. She could have done that by throwing a switch. She could have done that by not opening the gate to begin with.

What about using the ghost-light to shut off the twilight

effect partway? This might be a wild guess, but it sounded like a solid guess. She had been allowing twilight into the world in a controlled fashion, but keeping the wilder Uncreation out. She had been harvesting twilight, gathering it.

Why had Adramelech built the darned thing? If his mission had been to secure the blueprints, there was no need to build a working model. He would have just rolled up the blueprints and stuck them under his armpit at a jaunty angle —or planted a microfilm in a hollow tooth if he wanted to be fancier about it—and go skipping gaily back to his headquarters here, where all the mermaids would throw him a party.

The pain helped me concentrate. Maybe this whole underwater city clouded a man's wits, or maybe I was just painfully stupid.

Practically the last thing Dad had said to me was to promise to stop Achitophel Dreadful. To stop him *before he wraps himself in the Twilight again.*

Had Penny been gathering twilight for Adramelech to wrap himself in?

Dad's words came echoing in my memory: *Twilight is a side-effect of the Uncreation, and a dangerous one. A practitioner can use it to excuse himself from certain laws of nature in a limited way.*

Dad had also said: *I have to stop him before he brings the stars down.*

Adramelech himself had boasted of powers which the fools confining him in the asylum could not begin to understand. He had escaped using the art called *ylemsippur* in Ursprache. The shadow-wisdom. Shadowmages took control of the Oobleck, the *ylem*, which was the primal darkness before creation; a substance that allowed a warlock to bend or break certain laws of nature.

A substance currently in my bloodstream, left over from

when I had been dunked in the stuff, and drank it, breathed it, had it seep in through my pores.

What Foster had said returned to me: *Adramelech was losing his mind... Exposure to twilight will do that to you... I was supposed to stop the Professor from opening a Dark Gate in case he betrayed us. Which he did.*

The stuff was in me. Maybe I was going mad. I almost hoped so. Might be a relief.

I had not known enough, then, to ask what the difference between a Dark Gate and a normal gate was. Obviously, this was the term for a gate with no mate: a window into raw Uncreation. A place called the Twilight (Capital 'T') which was where the substance, or the side effect, called the twilight (small 't') came from. And this was the source of Adramelech's power as well as the thing driving him insane.

Foster had also mentioned Penny: *Her mission was to rescue Ossifrage. What she was doing on Earth, no one knows.*

Which meant Penny had cooperated with Adramelech. Which meant she had betrayed the Wisecraft. She was in trouble. I had helped her, so I was in trouble. Alexei had just vowed not to let me get imprisoned, not by anyone, which meant my trouble would make trouble for him, for Dad, for the alliance talks between Wisecraft and Ecclesia.

So it was all my fault after all. Alexei had been right.

Just then, I was glad I had bitten my tongue off because the pain distracted me from an even greater pain that bit into my soul like a pickaxe.

Because all this meant one more thing.

I spat again, wiped my chin, called my blood and torn bits back into my mouth—all the mermaids winced or gasped at the sight—and then I spoke.

"Adramelech knew my foolish dreams. He and I were close; we spoke often. He knew how badly I wanted to be a hero—to have some chance some day to do some great deeds. He saw my weakness. He used it to trick me. To make a fool of me. He sent me a note. I raced to the Haunted Museum, thinking I could save your sister. But she was in no danger."

That was not the most painful part of it. That I was a fool was not the most painful part.

Worse was this: it was so obvious, so blindingly obvious, what a fool I'd been, me, with my silly dreams of being a hero and winning a girl.

But to admit the obvious would have required me to admit my dream, my lifelong dream, the beautiful, magical, precious dream was... was...

Such a dream! A dream of doing deeds so wonderful and so legendary that girls would stop seeing my sloping fore-head, oversized jaw, big horse teeth, and squinty, little pig-eyes. My lifelong dream! Now I was within inches of achieving it! Now I had a magical sword. I had a charmed life. I had monsters to kill and a girl to save...

Now that I had everything I'd ever, ever dreamed, just now, when it was all so close... as close as the luscious fruit about to touch the lips of Tantalus in Hell...

That thought broke off in a fragment. It was almost too painful to think.

Almost. I forced myself to finish the thought, to look at it.

To see and to confess the obvious would have called on me to confess my dream was false and my life was hollow.

So I simply did not see it.

Why did I trust the Mad Professor? Dad told me not to trust him. Foster told me. Penny told me. They all told me that Professor Dreadful was insane, or dangerous, or treaso-nous. But I never allowed myself to rip up the bandage of those words and look at the wound beneath.

Like my Dad, like Foster, like Penny... the Professor had lied to me.

All the studious, steady work I did in the Haunted Museum; and every time I pulled an extra shift or swapped a joke to make him smile; and each lazy afternoon when the place was empty, but for the two of us, and the setting sun would send dusty red rays against the glass cases and stuffed heads on the far wall, and then the Professor would laugh in defiance at the lack of patrons and not let me lock the door until the clock in the entryway chimed the final chime of six o'clock; and the last, solemn conversation I had with him, when he took the Gideon Bible out of the hotel dresser drawer, and I knelt; that very hour when he anointed me with the oil of heroism and given me my life's mission; and everything else he did for me, large or small, or I did for him; all we shared, down to the last iota... it was all a lie.

I should have seen through the lie, and I would have, had I only been honest.

Had I only stopped flattering myself. Had I acted like a sober man instead of an infatuated, fatheaded, half-intoxicated teen.

God forgive me.

Silence hung in the wide, shadowy chamber with its floor of warm ice and its roof of rippling water.

Psamathe asked me the last question I would have ever expected. "Did Adramelech tell you to tell an untruth?"

3. Soul-Extracting Lama

I thought back. "Not in so many words. He told me to swear an oath to keep a secret from my father. A secret it was wrong to keep. I broke that oath."

Psamathe nodded. "This was cleverly devised by Adramelech. Wrongful silence or wrongful speaking, either one, would have darkened your soul and made you visible to what hungers for souls in the darkness. Adramelech knew also that your deeds thereafter would be seen and foreseen by the Dark Tower, including your thoughts, words, and deeds toward Parthenope, whom you rushed to save: as soon as you beheld or bespoke her, the protection her familiar granted her would be penetrated and she taken."

The thought that the liver-spotted, thin-boned, rheumy-eyed greybeards in the Dark Tower in another dimension were reading my dirtiest thoughts about Penny before I did was not only spooky and sad, but it was also shameful. I resolved to go to confession as soon as I could.

I said, "And I walked right into it. I wanted to rescue a girl. Instead, I endangered her. It is like she said." I shook my head.

I remember joking with other scouts in my troop about how we could all get life-saving merit badges by shoving each other into a pitfall or shark tank or by being thrown into the path of a speeding ambulance. We laughed because it was absurd to think of getting a medal for rescuing someone from a peril you create. But this is exactly what I had done.

Psamathe no doubt saw my twitching face as I tried to control my expression. She spoke in kind tones. "Do not be grieved that Adramelech deceived you! He deceived me and sisters older and wiser than I."

I had been staring at my feet. I looked up. Psamathe's face was lovely as ever, but now there was a real softness there. Compassion? Maybe so.

She continued, "We thought Adramelech to be a practitioner of the arts of necromancy and geomancy from Mizraim, from a land called Chemet, whose pharaohs serve the Dark Tower. It is not so: He is what is called a 'p'o-'bo, a Soul-Extracting Lama. He is from a land called Ladakh in Kunlun-Shan, in the aeon once called Pha, now called Aval-okitesvara, in honor of the grace of all the countless dead.

"Servants of the Dark Tower, the Nagual of Viracocha,

over many years erected the stepped pyramids and monuments in the deserts and wastelands of Pha. They slew men, mothers, virgins, and children of the aeon of Pha in hideous rites to beguile the powers of the unseen world: mocking gods, extracting beating hearts and gathering skulls, eating human flesh, flaying corpses, and dancing in robes made of the skins of the unquiet dead. The Nagual accomplished a catastrophic ritual called the *Nahui Aa*, the Apocalypse of the Wailing Sun.

"Nothing survived. Even the priests in their feathered cloaks who had accomplished the rite, maddened by opium, wearing as masks the flayed faces of their victims, their teeth bright red and grinning, vomiting the human blood on which they had overgorged, were swept away, dissolved to nothingness.

"The aeon of Pha was murdered.

"The unhoused spirits of men and beasts, and also the spirits of stone and tree, mountain, river, ocean, sun and star, in their countless myriads, and myriads of myriads, were obliterated utterly by the Dark Tower.

"The voices of the slain haunt the dreams of many worlds, so great is the death when an aeon dies. Nature and all the goddesses of nature, great and small, from eldest Mother Night to the smallest nymph or dryad, all perished."

It was a sobering image.

I said, "So what was he doing on Earth? Albion? Why use me to expose Parthenope?"

Psamathe said, "Some clue in your testimony, meaningless to you but not to us, might allow us a clear answer to that question. Please speak freely."

I said, "Let me see Parthenope first, please."

More quickly than the light from a snuffed candle, Psamathe's compassionate look vanished. "Parthenope is not the only Artabtatitae among the Wise, nor are bird shadows our sole means of deceiving the omniscience of the Dark Tower. Were it not so, all our striving against the foe would have been vain from the first. This crucial convocation at which we now toil is warded and hidden, or so we hope. But if your coming here was seen and foreseen by the Dark Tower, all those wards are penetrated. You expose us all to enemy eyes, even now, just as you exposed her then."

I said nothing.

She said, "Do not think us unjust or unwelcoming. But we seek to know how you escaped the tower none escape. By what means did you cheat their foreknowledge?"

I shook my head.

Her tone grew sharp, but not less lovely. "Because if you have no answer, the answer is that the enemy allowed you to escape as foreseen because it was foreseen, and all we do here and now is no more than the play of puppets whose strings are pulled by an unseen hand."

I answered nothing.

"Who hid you from the stars? Tell me!"

A sense of dread came over me.

Maybe it was something I saw in her eyes.

Maybe there was something about this gentle, pastel-tinted undersea city of pure pleasure and feminine delight, down here so deep in the sea where the sun never came, which was just as creepy and just as deadly as the dark and iron cruelties of the proud and ghastly tower reaching in all its terrible strength equally far up in to dead vacuum, where nothing lived.

Maybe beautiful seductresses whose fluid laws permit all things and who can sing you into hypnotic trances, maybe they were just as bad as crazy old Babylonians astrologers who knew your future down to the last ironclad, predeter-mined detail.

Or maybe not. These were enemies of the Dark Tower. Allies. Friendlies.

I did not care. That last question was a little too pointed. Psamathe was asking about Abanshaddi. But why had Parthenope not introduced them to each other?

A stab of guilt made me wince. I had been so worried about Parthenope all this time. I had not asked about little Abby or big Knack. (You would think I would look out for the other big, ugly guy, wouldn't you?) But Parthenope's was the only one whose name I was willing to utter aloud. If the mermaids did not know who I was, maybe they did not know who my companions were.

Foster was one of their own, of course, but what about the others? Without a translator, the mermaids could not talk to Nakasu, or to Ossifrage, and...

A thought struck me. I turned and looked at Alexei. How many minutes had he been standing there without speaking?

I looked again to where Psamathe sat on her throne and met her regal gaze. "Noble lady, why did you ask my name when you knew it?"

Psamathe said. "To suspect is not to know. Our reports listed you as dead. You are the son of Vseslav Volkhvyevich Muromets, are you not? He is the Captain of the Templar contingent which your Supreme Sacred Congregation of the Holy Office has sent to honor your emissaries to us.

"As I see you have guessed," she continued, smiling, "I asked your brother here, not for his tongue, but for his face, knowing when he looked on you, his eyes would reveal you to us. He misdoubted you, and so, for a moment, I doubted.

"That you both forgot yourselves and quarreled dispelled all question. I have many sisters, and we have many squabbles also. You are his family.

"Nor did you say in whose name you come even though his terrible cross hangs at your neck, and the fingerbone of a dead man also—a dead man too powerful for my sisters to send away. You follow the unnamed god who calls it wicked to eat from the Tree of the Knowledge. He forbids you from enjoying carnal knowledge also. Sad! You will not truly know the life of Anthemoessa."

Psamathe frowned and continued. "You are stiff necked and suspicious of us, as perhaps we are of you. This will pass, and we will come to know each other better. Your brother, Sir Alyosha, can escort you to the incarnadine dome where the emissaries of your people are housed. We will see your sevenscore and ten wives sent thither presently."

Alexei shot me a sharp look. His lips moved without sound. *Wives?*

She rose to her feet. "Our foe is terrible, ancient, and all-seeing, and only by the carefree and natural love we bear each other can we prevail over their most unnatural and deadly hate. Go and speak with your father, Vseslav the Seer! Mayhap you will tell him what you hide, and he will tell us. Go to your father!"

All the ladies curtseyed or knelt, and even the giant snake lowered its head. A column of water from the overhead volume lowered itself through the cloud of luminous bubbles. She stepped through the surface and into the column. Psamathe slid upward through the waters, graceful as a sea lion, even as the stalactite of water drew itself up into the glittering, unsteady roof.

Had I been allowed another question, I would have asked: *Are you sure he is my father?*

But she would not have had an answer to that question any more than did I.

8

MILITIA OF THE CHURCH MILITANT

1. Nine Popes

loating to one side of the vast central globe of the citadel, like a globular cluster of stars orbiting the galactic core, hung a grapebunch of spheres gleaming in hues of darker and lighter blue, azure, cerulean, slate-blue, and indigo. These surrounded a large glass orb, wider than a cathedral dome, the color of pink rose petals. A vast pocket of air surrounded the cluster.

Transparent streams snaked through gulfs of air to this pink dome. Within, beneath dozens of floating rose-red lamps like captive suns, was a lake toward which the airy streams fell as slender waterfalls. From the lowest point of the lake another stream, like the stem on a leaf, or maybe like the drain on an invisible bathtub, carried a waterfall away. What held countless cubic miles of water in midair, allowing it to flow upward or downward with cheerful disregard of gravity yet without expanding into a shapeless cloud, was a miracle I no longer questioned. I was brooding on other things.

On the lake was an object that came from a different world. For one thing, it was square and angular, like nothing else I had seen in this city of globes and curves and sinuous canals. For another, it was made of wood, a substance I had not seen used here at all.

She was a barge as large as an oil tanker but prettier than a jewelry box. She was twin hulled, like a catamaran, but the hulls were flat-bottomed and flat-keeled, not streamlined. A single deck stretched between the two hulls, like the flat top of an aircraft carrier. Her deck was made of dark and light woods, polished like a king's dining table, so that the wood shined like the facets of a gem. She had neither sail nor rudder, wheel nor screw. She was a ship meant to be towed or to drift, not to sail.

In two square towers port and starboard rose the ship's superstructure. Flags and shields displaying the red cross of the crusaders hung from the starboard tower. On the deck were knights and men-at-arms in the white surcoats and scarlet crosses of the Templars, dressed in the same futuristic armor as my brother, with sword, railgun, and folding-stock submachinegun.

From the port tower hung shields and banners blazoned with the crossed keys of St. Peter. Here was a second group of soldiers, pikemen dressed in puffy-shouldered Renaissance doublets and pantaloons of yellow and blue stripes above red tunics and leggings. They wore white gloves, wide white ruffs, and black steel morions with red plumes. This was the distinctive uniform of the Pontifical Swiss Guard.

My brother exchanged salutes with an officer in the yellow, blue, and red doublet and pantaloons getup whose name and rank I did not catch. I was wrapped in my own dark thoughts. Alexei was describing my situation and asking what to do with me; the Swiss Guard said to take me to the seneschal of the Templars since my being here was a military rather than a clerical matter.

As we walked away, Alexei said, "I am just trying to get you squared away. A bunk and a mess-hall pass."

"Why bother? I cannot die by starvation," I said morosely. "I tried."

"What?"

I was not in the mood to talk about me at that moment. So I raised my head and said. "I thought Swiss Guard all had to be Swiss. From Switzerland. That guy was Chinese."

"Don't let Captain Genpachi hear you say that. He's Japanese. The Archbishop of the Nagasaki Church sent him with Cardinal Shukeshiko as an honor guard to show that the Pope backs everything Shukeshiko says."

"Our Pope?"

"The Nagasaki Pope."

"From a parallel world?"

He nodded.

"How many Popes are there?"

"Nine, if you count the Metropolitan of the Jerusalem Church from Acre."

"Must cause arguments."

"Except for ours, all these Churches put aside their differences centuries ago, gathered bishops from all the worlds, held a curia, and elected a Pope fair and square."

"What is different about ours?"

"Do you remember in our history when there were three rival popes who all excommunicated each other?"

I said, "The Great Western Schism. 1378 to 1417."

"It was resolved by the Council of Constance. Everyone eventually got back together. All the followers of Christ actually listened to Christ's prayer that we all keep His church unified as one." Now he grimaced. "What makes our world different is that Earth stopped doing that, more or less.

141

There are differences in rite and ritual and even doctrine between the parallel versions of history. Maybe seeing a common enemy bent on your destruction puts those differences in their proper perspective."

"So which Church is running all the Churches?"

"The Assyrian Church of Sasan is in charge. The Second Coming happened on their world pretty early on, and they created the *Consistorium Ecclesia* in the first place. But Nagasaki is in charge of this embassy because they have better relations than anyone else with Hawaiki, who arranged the meeting."

"Who is Hawa-icky?"

"A place, not a person. It is the sacred island of an aeon called Uenuku. In our world, Hawaiki sank. We call it Lemuria. The Uenuku witch-doctors are part of the Wisecraft. They want to get together with us and use the 'White-Christ Magic' to smite the Dark Tower."

"Are they the guys who turn into fish? I've heard of them."

By then, we were belowdecks.

2. Imprisoned, Again

This place was like a palace, with sweeping staircases, not ladders, and carven double doors rather than oval hatchways. The passageways were wide as pillared halls but gloomy as a cathedral at night. Everything was lit with candle-racks and chandeliers, or candles winking behind sapphire or ruby glass. It took my eyes a while to adjust to the soft, butter-yellow constellations of gathered candle flames after the eerie, bioluminous lamps of the mermaids.

In the candlelight, the deckboards were as brightly polished as a mirror. Everything was oak, mahogany, teak, and cherry, not the woods normally used for ships. Wainscoting and moulding was intricately carved and gilded with acanthus or oak leaf motifs, lilies, and roses. Little ivory statuettes of patriarchs, saints, and angels stood in small nooks to either side. Usually, you can tell who they are supposed to be by what they are holding or stepping on, but, for some reason, I recognized none of the iconography, except for the smiling maiden in a veil trampling a snake. Panels adorning bulkheads and overheads were painted or scrimshawed with biblical and classical scenes of myths, miracles, or martyrdoms, the Fall of Lucifer, or the Fall of Troy.

I noticed that, splendid to the eye as this interior might seem, it was actually austere. We passed a barracks. The bedding was stiff mats on a hard deck; each pillow, a block of wood. We took a shortcut through the mess hall. The diners sat on benches of wood. There were no electric lights, no water fountains, no little signs pointing to the men's room. I was reminded of how the most beautifully decorated church was never comfortable: no pews had cushions.

We passed men in black wool cassocks with scarlet silk rabats. The cardinals wore white sashes, the bishops wore purple, and the prelates and protonotaries wore black. Canons, beneficiaries, deacons, and seminarians each had distinctive uniforms. There seemed to be some buzz of excitement pestering them, for they walked quickly, if quietly, and spoke in urgent voices, if soft.

Alexei approached a figure in white armor seated on a folding leather stool. His table was a wooded plank set across two sawhorses and draped in linen. A propane lantern stood here, blazing and hissing. Paper, inkwell, blotter, and parchment were strewn haphazardly about. His submachinegun was being used as a paperweight. The bowl of his helmet was an ashtray, into which he flicked white ash. He had a thick cigar with a potent scent gripped between this teeth. Alexei saluted, and the man flicked his eyes up and grunted.

Alexei spoke in Latin, "You are the Seneschal, now, Marshal? Where is everyone?"

The Marshal replied, "I am merely warming his seat. The Seneschal is with the Grandmaster at the Convocation, along with all the high-hats. You were supposed to be there ten minutes ago."

Alexei objected, explaining he had been waiting on Princess Psamathe. The superior cut him off. "She was supposed to be there, too, as head of the Circassian delegation. Let her explain her tardiness to her Queen. You answer to the Grandmaster. Off with you, son, double-time."

Alexei started away and called over his shoulder, "This is my brother, Ilya. He just came back from the dead and escaped the Dark Tower. See to him, please, Sir."

Then Alexei was gone, and I was alone again.

The Marshal returned writing a letter or whatever he was doing. I had been away from the mermaids for precisely one moment, and already was I missing having three or four beautiful girls ready and willing to stuff winegrapes in my mouth. They might be dangerous, but they did not ignore you.

Because of that, and other reasons, when the Marshal finally looked up from his writing and barked a few simple questions at me, I am afraid my answers were a little nonchalant.

Well, maybe they were a little snarky.

He told me to surrender my katana and would not listen to any of my reasons why I should not. Also, his Latin was no better than mine, so there may have been a misunderstanding. Also, when he doubted that I was an abomination of Cainem, I picked up the pen-knife he used to trim his cigars, and drove it through my own palm and out the back of my hand. I held it in front of his face and told him to take a good look. Maybe a little loudly. And there was another pikeman nearby who rushed into grab me. Then others who came to help him.

Maybe the pikeman thought I was threatening the Marshal, or maybe he wanted to render medical aid to my self-inflicted wound. Or maybe I am an idiot. I had a lot of options.

I found out that I was a lot less calm that I would have been back in Tillamook. I mean, if someone in the old days had tried to grab me and twist my arm behind my back, I doubt I would have dislocated my own shoulder on purpose, twisted my forearm around in a direction it could not possibly go, snapping a bone or two in the process, in order to grab the guy's surprised face with my fingers. I also had not been able to twist my head in a half-circle like an owl, snapping my neck vertebrae in the process, in order to grin a wicked grin in his face.

So I ended up losing my grandfather's magical werewolf-killing katana, and my Dad's utility belt, and flack jacket, and priceless relic, all my dignity and self-respect. Beneath my jacket, I wore nothing but a pair of red silk pantaloons Abby had found for me in the Chamber of Fated Rarities when we had recovered my lost sword.

Which was now lost again. I was once more under arrest, once more stripped of my gear. At least the Templars were decent about it. No one poked spears through me or threw me out of ten-thousand-foot-high trapdoors.

I was locked into a windowless cabin paneled and floored with polished wood and told to wait until someone or other decided my disposition. The place was gorgeous, with paintings on the bulkheads and a fresco adorning the overhead. As with everything here, it was overwhelmingly luxurious to the eye and hard and cold to the touch. There was no furniture aside from a cot, a stool, and an elaborate writing desk.

I asked for a meal and a priest. When I say I "asked," I

mean I yelled it at the white-armored Templars as they backed out of the cabin.

Slam. The door shut. Click. The lock locked. I was in a richly appointed but uncomfortable cabin with no porthole and no exit, lit by a single, solitary oil lamp.

Looking over the options, I decided on *idiot*.

I am a big boy. I did not cry. Wanted to. Didn't.

3. Father Susan

The guys I yelled at must have heard me, and they must have been in a nice mood. Or filled with Christian charity. Or something. Both food and a father confessor showed up.

The food came first. It was bread and fish. I am not sure if it were breakfast, lunch or dinner. No timepiece was in this cabin, no porthole in the hull, and neither sun nor moon this far down below the sea. After I was done easting. Japanese priest the size and shape of a sumo wrestler knocked politely at my door.

His face was very round, and his eyes grew so narrow when he smiled, which was often, that they were mere slits. The man was enormous enough in girth and width of chest to pass for a monster like Nakasu, with his hair oiled and folded into a small topknot peering down over his shaven skull. He waddled on silent feet, moving his great bulk with unexpected delicacy.

With him was a brass statue dressed in the uniform of a Swiss Guard. I did not see how the joints worked since the elbows and knees were covered with his blousy sleeves or balloonish leggings. The head and hands were brass, and his footfall clanged on the deck.

The father politely asked me to promise not to hurt anyone. Then, he shooed the brass statue out of the cabin. The animate being seemed reluctant to leave, squinting distrustfully at me with the featureless ball-bearings it wore in its metal eyesockets, but the father insisted gently but firmly, and closed the door.

The Father spoke Latin with no accent, but with a slight singsong voice that was pleasant to the ear. His voice was so high pitched, and his girth so big, that I imagined he was filled with helium. He sat in the cabin's only chair while I perched on the edge of the hard cot.

"I am Father Susan-no-O," he said. "You are the son of the Turcopolier, Vseslav the Seer?"

To myself, I admitted I was not sure which was more weird: that my father was a seer or that this big man was named Susan.

Aloud, I admitted I did not know what a turcopolier was.

"Ah. So. The Turcopolier is the Third Master of the Order, after the Grandmaster, and the Seneschal. He commands the mounted archers, aeronauts, and native contingents as well as the sergeant brothers for the Templar commandry. You father only recently came into this high position."

"I am adopted," I said bitterly. "So I am not his son. I am from his world."

"Do they have homunculi on your world?" He nodded toward the brass-faced apparition, who was even now peering in suspiciously through a round and slatted widow in the door. "Talos is possessed of artificial imitation of life, and it can neither speak nor reason. It knows obedience and disobedience, like a loyal dog, but cannot know right from wrong."

It seemed an odd question. I said, "We have stories about such things. Usually involving mad scientists with German names, like Frankenstein."

"That is fitting," he said, nodding. "It hails from the aeon called Togarmah, which the common people call Midas.

Their Pope is Archbishop of Salzburg, titled Primate of Germany. In the aeon of Acre, the Jerusalem Church, they discovered how to give souls and free will to the Spartoi, their artificial men, so as to undo the abomination of making them; we are hoping to nurture a similar miracle here. Have you such things in your world?"

"Only in movies."

"Ah? So...?"

"Moving pictures. Like a magic lantern show. We have technology in Albion, jets and computers. But no artificial life. No magic. Just in stories."

"Aside from moving pictures? I see." He nodded. "The things of your world are stories in ours: tales about flying machines and thinking machines. You are from one of the aeons who shoot fireworks to the moon, carrying men on its nose, yes?"

"We have moonrockets, yes."

He grinned with pleasure. "Amazing! Tiras, Brennus, and Midas also have sailed ships to the moon or founded colonies in the sky."

"Apparently, we are also the only world with abortion."

He asked me what that was. I shook my head and said, "Never mind what that is. They already locked me in here because I am an abomination from Cainem. I do not want you to get worse ideas about us."

His eyebrows, when he raised them, traveled an alarming distance up across the dome of his shaved pate. "You were locked in here because you lost your temper and made a ruckus. You surrendered to the sins of wrath and despair, both of which offend the most merciful Virgin. The solitude was to give you time to collect your thoughts. Although, honestly..." he dropped his voice to a whisper and said, "The people from Albion do make the rest of us open our eyes and perspire cold perspiration, perhaps."

"We make you nervous? Why?"

"In your world, the Universal Church is seated in Rome, not Constantinople."

"And?"

"Rome is the city of the Romans, who hung Our Savior cruelly on a cross. How strange that the Lord would save those who hate Him! Yet in other worlds, no Messiah yet has come as promised. In others yet, no promise was made."

"Then there are many Christs, one for each world? How can that be if he is the only begotten Son? Wasn't one crucifixion in one world enough for all the rest?"

"He is the same in all worlds," said the huge man in his thin voice. "Men differ. Some men chose life. Some death. In Rhodanim, Christ was given a crown in Jerusalem by the Jews, not condemnation, but Vespasian slew him as a rebel and tore the Temple down. Both were restored in three days. In Gomer, Herod found and slew him as a child, but being raised again, his shed blood cured the world. In Javan, he was stoned and hung on a tree. His second advent there is very near, for the sun has lost its strength, and unclean spirits walk abroad. In Sasan, the Golden City is clearly seen, even by the blind, as a sign and a wonder, for the reign of a thousand years of peace is soon there to begin. That world was blessed with a second advent."

I scowled. That did seem strange. Why did God make some worlds better than others? It did not seem fair.

That led to another thought. "Was Christ Japanese in your world?"

"No, Jewish, as in yours."

"How did the Pope end up in Japan in your world?"

He said, "Atheist republics in France, Germany, and Russia fought against Christian kings of Britain, Spain, Italy, and Japan in a war that drenched the globe with blood. The Holy City was cursed and rendered uninhabitable by the

Atheists, who killed one hundred million souls. During the fighting, the Curia and all the Metropolitans, Cardinals, and Archbishops who declined the honor of martyrdom fled to Japan."

Father Susan-no-O smiled in a self-satisfied way. "Prophets sing that the people will return, rejoicing. Each man will come, carrying his tools on his shoulder. All will gather from their scattering and come to the ruins. We will rebuild the city stone by stone, and raise the gates again. Japan is only the host for now. In my world, Japan has been a Christian nation since the Shimabara Uprising. Do you know of it?"

"No, I've never heard of it. Maybe it never happened in my world."

"Shiro Amakusa was a Christian and a miracle-worker in the Edo period. He led the peasants to overthrow the usurpations of Tokugawa even though all the world said the poor and meek were powerless before the Shogun. He was betrayed by the wicked Yamada, and Shiro was beheaded, and his head was displayed on a pike in Nagasaki. But, as he said he would, he returned from the dead, picked up his head, and carried it in his hands. Head in one hand and spear in the other, he gathered the people and the *ronin* against the army."

I said, "How is that possible?"

He said, "You doubt? Could you yourself not do the same?" And, when I had no answer, he said, "Shiro baptized the Empress Meisho, who took the name Francesca. Later, he baptized the Sea-Dragon princess Otohime, who took the name Magdalena. It is a great victory for the Church to baptize a pagan goddess. You see why Nagasaki is famed. My world has many more reports of miracles than any other Christian world."

I said, "In my world, we bombed Nagasaki with a terrible weapon."

"How queer! Parallel history has many odd ironies."

4. Brother World, Sister Star

A silence fell. I have noticed that other people often rush to fill up silence with words when a conversation lapses, but not priests. I wondered why.

I said, "Father, if history is God's will, how can it be so different for different worlds? Aren't there some aeons where Christ has not come? Does the Almighty will those worlds to be damned?"

I did not say it aloud, but I was wondering about my real father, whom I had never met. Was my real Dad a creature like Rahab? A monster whose only joy was inflicting pain?

It occurred to me that he was still alive. Come to think of it, no matter how long it was, my blood relations in Cainem were still alive: brothers, sisters, cousins. They would never die. They would not be slender, handsome, and blond like Alexei and Dobrin; not slender, gorgeous, and blonde like my cousins Alyonushka and Zabava. They would be dark-haired, bulky, bristly, and thick. They would be people who looked like me.

Cainem was a world without Moses, or David, or Mary, or Christ. It had no Ten Commandments, no Psalms, no Gospels. A damned world.

But could they be damned if they never died? But anyone alive on the world's last day would still come before the judgment, wouldn't he? Come Doomsday, everyone gets resurrected, don't they? And never die again. The damned are thrown into the Lake of Fire prepared for the Devil and his angels. But the fire will not kill you.

We will all be of the host who yearns for death in vain on that day.

I covered my face in my hands. It all seemed too much. Things had gone too far. My Dad had lied to me. The Professor. My best friend Foster. Yes, I had even lied to myself, telling myself I was a champion, a rescuer, a hero, a superstar.

Everything was a lie. I was told that God was great and kind and loving. Was that a lie?

Why did worlds like mine exist if God was so great? Why the Dark Tower and all its witchcraft and slave camps and instruments of torture? Where was the Christ of that world? Or did only the blond people get offered the chance to be saved?

Father Susan-no-O spoke softly. "*Have I any pleasure at all that the wicked should die? saith the Lord God: and not that he should return from his ways and live?* I do not know why the different aeons have different histories. For that matter, I do not know why different men have different lives. Some are just and kind but die in poverty, pain, and loneliness; while others are cruel and foolish but die peacefully in bed, surrounded by sons and daughters, who will revere and laud his name for generations. Each man's story is different. Each world has a different history. But I know the ending is always the same."

I looked up, "What ending?"

"Death, followed by judgment, followed by Heaven or Hell."

I nodded morosely.

He said, "Heaven is waiting for those meek enough to ask Heaven to enter them; Hell for those too proud to ask for the help to escape it. And yet all these worlds are our brothers, all the stars our sisters, for they were fashioned, as were we, by the same hand."

A dark rage that was within me suddenly bubbled up. "You don't understand! My father—or the man I thought was my father—told me my mother was dead. The woman I thought was my mother. But he lied, and she is alive! I just found out that my brother does not know that even though he knows all about me, my real world, my real family! Who are my real father and mother? For all I know, it was Rahab! I fed him to a bloodquaffer!"

Then, I realized I was shouting. I mumbled that I was sorry, and I looked around for a handkerchief and wiped my nose and eyes on my sleeve.

Father Susan-no-O learned forward and touched me on the knee. "*Who is my mother? and who are my brethren? And he stretched forth his hand toward his disciples and said, 'Behold my mother and my brethren!'* Our Lord was troubled by the same question that troubles you. Is fatherhood a thing of flesh and blood? Or is it a thing of the spirit?"

"Adopting me did not change my nature. I am still an abomination."

Father Susan-no-O shook his head slowly. "If adoption cannot make us sons of the father, then what hope is there for the Japanese? Or any gentile? How can we inherit the covenant of Abraham or of the Messiah? But if fatherhood is of the spirit, let each man do what he must to be a good son."

His voice, as I said, was soft and high pitched. I suppose, if I were being honest, I would say it was a silly voice. But when he said those words, they sounded like they came from the core of the world. My goal to be a hero had turned me into a goat, not a hero. What if my goal were something simpler? What about being a good son?

With this thought, words and tears started spilling out of me. Father Susan asked me to kneel, and he bent his head to listen carefully.

9

THIRD MASTER OF THE ORDER

1. Vseslav the Seer

I was on my knees, praying, when my Dad came in, smiling. His eyes were shining with joy.

With him was a second man. His mantle was black and bore a red cross on breast and back. His beard was dark red, his hair was light red, and his eyes were red. I do not mean his eyes were bloodshot, I mean the irises of his eyes were the hue of a ruby. He had a long bundle tucked under one arm, which he carefully placed on the writing desk. He saluted Father and stepped backward out of the cabin, closing the door.

I never found out his name. Father simply called him "sergeant."

As for me, Father Susan had given me many hard words to think over. Like a hardtack biscuit, I had to chew them over before I could swallow them. But the penance he had imposed was harder yet: to obey my father. And to say three paternosters.

But a sense of deep calmness, even serenity, was now

inside me. The Oobleck, that nasty stuff, which clearly was still infecting me, as it turned out, could pick up and amplify good moods as well as bad. An hour of prayer had turned the goo in my bloodstream into something light, refreshing, airy, and even-tempered. Now I had a double reason to avoid the temptation to give in to lust or to anger or to any hasty, rash emotion. That, and the creepy idea that old men in the Dark Tower had read any thought I might be thinking years before I thought it.

So I stood, saying, "Father, I have failed you. I sinned against you and against Heaven. You sent me to shut off the Moebius Gate in the Haunted Museum, but instead, thanks to me, the Earth has been invaded..."

He hugged me so tightly it knocked the wind out of me. He then shoved me back so he could hold me at arms length and just stare. He was grinning like I had never seen. Tears were in his eyes.

"You were dead," he said. "And now you are alive!"

The old anger which I thought I had quenched stirred in my guts. "You know I can never die."

He said, "I thought you fell into the Uncreation. There are no boundaries, no shore, no directions, no laws of nature. I thought there was no way back."

I said, "Wouldn't that mean I was lost, out of reach, out of sight forever, not dead?"

He wiped his eyes. "That is all death is. Really. Our loved ones sleep, or they wait for us in the next world. They still exist, but they are no longer near us. Out of sight forever, like you said. Losing you in the ocean was the same as that." Father shook his head wearily.

"Worse, in a way," I said. "Because I never die, I never go to Heaven, so we won't be together there."

Once again, strangely, I saw that look in his eye I had never seen as a child. Fear for me.

He spread his hands. "When you were gone, I blamed myself. I put you into danger thinking you could survive anything. What a fool I was! Yes, technically, an immortal boy lost forever in an endless abyss would be alive, but so what? I live my life forever separated from my wife. Now I had done the same thing to my child, my poor, silly, unhappy little foundling!"

He paused to wipe his eyes. This was all unexpected. Usually, he is stern. I had never seen him actually explain himself before. He is not a man who shares his emotions.

I said, "You've changed."

He said, "You've grown. Ah! You have no idea what a pleasure and joy it was to raise you. Look at how you've turned out!"

"Joy? But I thought—I—"

"A little rough around the edges. Work in progress. Only to be expected. But every father I know would envy me."

"What? Why?"

"I raised a child who was never in danger of dying! If he swallows a paperclip, wedges his head between the bars of his crib, chases a ball into traffic, falls from a tree, high-dives into the shallow end of the neighborhood swimming pool, or has an accident while target shooting, a deathless boy will simply get better. I cannot even start the list of all the things I never had to worry about. No dentist bills, for one thing. Wait until you have kids."

Since I doubted any woman alive would want to have kids that looked like me, I answered nothing.

"I am only sorry I was not stricter," he said. "I let you get away with things, and your brothers copied you. They were envious if I let you take risks I did not let them take. That stirred up some hard feelings between you three, and I am sorry about that."

Do you know how disorienting it is to find out you are

not an earthman? To discover that your father is not your father? Or to learn that the Catholic Church since the Middle Ages has been fighting the Tower of Babel in alien, monster-filled, parallel aeons of history but has kept the whole thing utterly secret? Well, I know exactly how disorienting such things are.

This was worse. My whole universe did a backflip and landed on its head.

My picture-perfect fashion-model handsome brothers envied me? Me?

My athletic, skillful, and super-intelligent straight-A brothers? Dobrin, who did everything right the first time? Alexei, who did everything right the first time and also cracked jokes?

Dobrin was our local rock star, or at least our local folk singer, and could charm girls with romantic ballads on his guitar. He had been dating Lorie Pine since he turned fifteen. She was the cutest girl in town, captain of the cheerleader squad, prom queen, and head of every other after-school club and activity. Alexei had a different girlfriend every six months, and he treated them all like pests, yet they still swarmed around him. They envied me?

The next surprise was bigger. Dad threw back the leather flap of the bundle on the writing table. Here was the sharkskin scabbard and katana of Grandpa Mikhail, Dancing Maiden. The flak jacket was there as was the utility belt.

"It's all my gear!" I said. Then, I corrected myself. "All your gear."

"Not mine. Yours. As of now," he said. "A Confirmation gift. You are a man. Congratulations. I have put in the paperwork to have you enrolled in the Order."

I was blinking like an owl in sunlight. "The order?"

"The Ancient and Honorable Order of the Poor Fellow-

Soldiers of Christ and of the Temple of Solomon. The Templars."

Me? All my dreams of being a hero, which had died half an hour ago, now came flooding back. To be a knight is a fine thing. To wear the red cross of the Crusade is even finer.

He said, "As a master of the cavalry and aeronauts, I also have authority to enroll a child as a squire as well as the authority to knight squires on the battlefield as a reward for exemplary courage and skill above the call of duty. I did both to you."

"What are you talking about? You did not knight me."

"The report I gave the Grandmaster says I did. That means that what you did was done under my authority as Turcopolier."

"What did I do? Aside from letting an invasion fleet from Ur land in our world and sink California into the sea? All those deaths are on my head."

"Don't talk nonsense."

"Alexei said you were in trouble, and it was my fault."

"Hmm. I was charged with making certain that when twilight gathered on Neahkahnie Mountain, the ossuary beneath the cursed monastery of Acarna opened, that nothing of the *outreterre*, the otherworlds, broke into ours." He sighed. "Having a full-scale invasion in force was indeed a failure of my duty; my superiors charged me with neglect for sending an untrained and uniformed boy to secure a Moebius coil allegedly built by Achitophel of Mizraim.

"When I pointed out that there was no one else to send," he continued, "and that I had trained you your whole life for this, the Board of Inquiry blamed my lack of forethought and provision for not having men standing by. But no one foresaw what Professor Dreadful meant to do, no more than did I. We all believed the wards around our world were fool-proof. His machine simply should not have worked. By every known law of metaphysical engineering, it could not have worked!"

"So I am to blame."

"The responsibility is mine, not yours. You were kept in the dark. You did not know..."

"I knew what to you said to do. I knew the task. Stop the Moebius coil. It did not get done."

He laughed aloud. "You have the right attitude! But don't beat yourself up. You've already done more, and in less time, than a whole regiment. I wanted to have the Grandmaster here to debrief you since we don't have time to go through normal channels, but it turns out we do not even have time for that. Things are moving quickly. The Convocation may reach a decision today. If the Wise are as wise as their name suggests, they will agree."

"Decision on what?"

He clapped me on the shoulder.

"To take you with us, of course!" It was rare to see him grin. "To complete the mission you started!"

2. Sasan or Cush?

"Jonah the Pteropher is the name of the man you rescued." Dad continued. Jonah? I did not correct him since I was sure I could not pronounce Abby's name for the guy. This was the man I had been calling Ossifrage. Dad said, "He is the only one whose prayers can stir to life the Colossus. That is the..."

I said, "I know. A prayer-powered mecha? A giant robot?"

"A silly way to describe it, but, yes, something like that. But it is older than the universe, so it does not have a nativity, which means it does not have a horoscope. The Dark Tower cannot foretell its movements. We have it in Tharaka, but we cannot run it. Cannot even raise it out of the ground. It is fused into the bedrock. The witches can run it, but they don't have it. It is the perfect opportunity for our two groups to work together. There is a lot of reflected enmity between our timelines."

What he meant by "reflected enmity" was not hard to guess. The witches were the bad guys defeated in our history, as the churchmen were in theirs. Each had exterminated the parallel versions of the other in our home aeon.

It seemed strange to hold a grudge against people who had never done anything against you, merely against something like twin brothers not actually related to you. But then again, I had met a lot of people mad at the Catholic Church over things no one had ever done to them, like the Spanish Inquisition, or had never been done at all, like Galileo being put on trial for science. I had heard of people who hated Jews, for example, and blamed them for everything under the sun; but I had never heard of people who hated the Germans even though everything wrong in history, from the fall of the Roman Empire to World War One to the Holocaust could be laid at their doorstep, if you wanted to play the game of blaming groups for what their ancestors did.

I said, "Foster said the McGuffin armor was in Cush. Or maybe he said Sasan. Actually, I think he said both. Penny insisted on heading to Cush. Now it is in Tharaka?"

Dad said, "No, Sasan is where it is headed, the target. Tharaka is a kingdom in Cush, south of Egypt along the Nile."

I said, "But you said we had it, in our territory. Cush is a Wisecraft aeon. I thought it was their main place, their capital."

"It is. The Wise have been fighting the Dark Tower since the fifth century and at least had been able to hold their own. They have suddenly run into a series of serious, uninterrupted defeats. The Dark Tower forced open a gate in Cush in the sixteenth century and established a beachhead. The

Strega of Cush asked us to send troops from Acre and Sasan, which we did, and in numbers enough to drive the Urrasse back. But when we freed the territory, we found Kushite and Coptic Christians, loyal to a prince named Prestor John, someone who, in our world, is nothing but myth. So everything south of Meroe, we did not turn back over to the Wise. Beyond the Sixth Cataract, beyond Soba. And that is where the Panoply is resting. In the middle of the kingdom of Prestor John."

"So they need your permission to get it."

"So we need to put aside old differences and cooperate. The Panoply is one of the few things we have good reason to believe the Dark Tower cannot see."

"Foster did not mention any of this. Were his own people keeping him in the dark?" I scowled. There seemed to be a lot of that going around.

"Could be." Dad looked sober. "I doubt the Wise of Cush would have told the Wise of Riphath exactly where the Panoply was. There is an internal power struggle going on between the strega and the nightriders, something—we are not sure what—concerning their whole approach to the whole war effort. The Bishops think it is crucial to aid the faction friendly to us and to make the joint venture a signal success in order to weaken the anti-clerical faction… You have a crucial role to play in this…"

3. Sister, Siren, Monster, Spy

It was not that I was not curious. I was. I really was. It was not that I did not enjoy that my secretive, close-mouthed father was actually willing to share the truth with me. For once. I really did.

It was just that there was something more important.

"Dad! Listen up! I came here with other people…"

It was really odd seeing him smile. His face was not really the right shape for it. It did not go with his Slavic scowl lines. "Of course! Your hundred wives? Not to worry. The Wisecraft and the Holy Office have already agreed to try to get the young ladies home—those whose worlds we can reach. And, as part of the corporal works of mercy, there are several Church societies to aid escaped slaves whose funds are available..."

I said, "Listen to me, for once, dammit!"

His face grew stern and remote, and his eyes turned cold. He was once again the father I knew from my youth. "Don't take that tone with me, young man! Anything you can say, you can say in a respectful..."

I lowered my voice. "Sir. Listen to me, please."

"Go on."

"The mermaids are holding my friends! The people who helped me escape. The ones I rescued from the Dark Tower. They won't let me see them! What if they are being tortured?"

The muscles in his jaw twitched. My guess is that he felt as I did. Mesmerism is worse than torture in its way. A man can resist torture. Or he can pray. But what can a man in a trance do?

All he said was: "Who is being held?"

"A young girl named Abanshaddi. She is a short and dark-haired tomboy thinner than a rail. A tall and headless Blemmyae named Kaqqudu Nakasu. He looks like the hairy monster from Bugs Bunny who wears tennis shoes. But without the hair. Or the shoes."

"Headless?"

"He is from another aeon. I don't remember the name. One where Ham was never cursed by Noah. "

His expressionless face grew more expressionless. For a moment, I thought he was angry at me. He was. But not at me. "This is not good. The Circassians told us it was no one but you and Jonah and a young lady of their royal family, an operative of theirs …"

I said, "That is Penny. Penelope Dreadful. Her real name is Parthenope."

"Our Penny? She is under arrest."

"What? Why?"

He opened the door and spoke a few words to the black-cloaked sergeant, who saluted, and jogged off.

Then, Father sighed and sat down on the couch, gesturing me toward the stool. "We're guests here. I cannot force the Wisecraft to do anything, but the Legate maybe can bring some pressure to bear. You are sure it was Penelope Dreadful? There is no possibility of mistake?"

"Come on, Dad. I have the covers of magazines taped to the wall above my bed with photos of her in her sailboat, smiling. I saw her every day at work after the Professor was arrested. Even a perfect disguise, if that is what you are thinking, would not have fooled me. I was closer to her than I am to you now, and we had lengthy and personal conversations on topics only she would know. And I was with her for…" I stopped, stumped.

How long had it been since I had found her in the harem chamber? One conversation, one fight, one running away, a freaky hairdo, a second fight in the entrance chamber, then we jumped into nowhither, ended up underwater in an abandoned enemy stronghold… Most of the time had been spent swimming, my lungs full of water, holding a glowing hoop.

"I was with her, in close quarters, for several hours. Half a day, tops." I said. It seemed longer. I also had no idea how long I had been under narco-hypnosis by the mermaids, being interrogated. Days? Weeks? I had no idea what date it was back on Earth.

He was saying, "We knew she was a spy when she moved into Tillamook. You remember Deacon Maugris?"

"The birdwatcher?" He had visited our house for two weeks a few Easters ago.

"He was actually a paladin of the Templars from Brennus. He brought a long-range animal magnetism lens that was supposed to be able to detect the different wavelengths of theurgistic energy. He observed her and concluded that Miss Dreadful was an Artabtatitae, a witch of the wild magic. It did not pick up any other vibrations. Assuming the galvanic sciences of the Gallic Church can do what they say, which sometimes I doubt. Besides, she has a familiar spirit, so that is why we ruled out her being a sea-witch. It's not a penguin."

"She sailed around the world by listening to the water. You didn't find that suspicious?"

"I did. That is why I got permission to have Sir Maugris and his theurgy-lens stationed at my house for a fortnight."

I said, "Well, she is a Renaissance Man of witchcraft, or so she said. She has water-bending and hypno-powers like a mermaid. And glow in the dark, if that is a power. She also called herself a *strega*." Why that name stuck in my mind, I don't know.

He made the sign of the cross. "Strega are the witches of Cush, the forest-world. They use dreams to foretell future events and can cast an astral body to remote locations."

I had not seen Penny do anything like that. I said, "You know about Wild Eyes, her pet. There is actually some sort of evil spirit inside. I can see it staring out through the bird's eyes. That type of witchcraft had a name, too. Theo-something." That name did not stick.

"Theriomancy. The wild magic. The witches of that world have familiar spirits called *fetches*, who can call forth animal-shades representing a man's soul or his fate. Fetches can also hunt ghosts and savage them."

"Also, her broomstick glows with *ylemaramu*. It's the blue light that…"

"Eosphormancy. Diurnal magic to banish twilight. It comes from Panchaea. That is a world where Hercules was never born, so the classical gods were wiped out by giants." He shook his head. "No wonder I was outflanked by her, not to mention by Achitophel. Your young lady is quite accomplished."

"Hercules?"

"Some of the miracles that split timelines include pagan miracles, yes."

I squinted. "How does that work, theologically speaking? If the classical gods are fallen angels, why would they be able… No! Never mind that now. Focus!" I drew a breath and continued, "Dad, I owe Knack my life, and I owe Penny a date. We are going to watch *To Have and to Have Not*. Why was she arrested?"

"Do you remember why I sent you to close the Moebius coil?"

4. My Last Night on Earth

"You said it might be giving off radiation. You meant the twilight effect."

"The effect stops gunpowder and electricity, but in greater concentrations…"

I cut him off. "Dad, I know all about it. You sent me because I could survive the effect. It would not kill me because I cannot die."

"And because there was nothing else I could have done. I could not have sent you to the cursed monastery, where the walls of the world were being broken open. You would not have known what to do. Achitophel of Mizraim used his necromantic arts to gather the twilight. All the animals in the forest near that mountain slope were dead.

"Had I been even ten minutes later, it would have been too late!" He continued. A dark look was in Dad's eye. It must have been a near thing. "He called into the Uncreation, and something that dwells there answered him. I heard it roaring in a voice like a waterfall. I drove it back with bell, book, and candle."

Dad shook his head wearily. "Achitophel, we knew, was a geomancer from Mizraim. He knows the art of measuring ley lines running between ancient monuments and holy or unholy ground. It is an Egyptian magic that allowed them to call upon the shadows of dead Pharaohs to bless and curse the land. Ghosts can, at times, stir up or becalm the twilight in certain ways. Nothing like what I saw. That was not some shade of an Egyptian King whose face started to form in the clouds above the mountain. It was older than anything human. He should not have been able to do that."

"Do what? What was he trying to do?"

Father shook his head. "No one knows. I know what he screamed at me when I shot him. He may have been raving. I hope he was."

"You shot him?"

The corner of his mouth twitched with embarrassment. I knew what the look meant; he had not set up the perfect kill-shot correctly, or he had pulled the trigger too early and only winged the target.

I forgot for a moment how much I liked the Professor and how relieved common decency said I should have felt. Instead, I clucked my tongue. "You botched the shot? What would Grampa Mikhail say?"

"I missed, or he is no longer something a bullet can kill. Either way, I did not find his body. It is safe to assume he is still alive. He was trying to unleash a weapon against the Dark Tower. An infinite weapon. An absolute weapon."

"Wait? You *stopped* him? Why?"

"You know how an atomic bomb is triggered by a primary? A hollow sphere of conventional explosives that makes the fissionable material implode?"

"Yes."

"Our whole world was his primary."

5. No More Lies

A sensation like a cold wind moved through my bones. I knew what Dad was talking about it. Psamathe had just described the same thing. Breaking all the laws of nature in a world and returning it to the primal, primordial, roaring storm of darkness that existed before God commanded light to exist.

Again, it was all stuff I wanted to know and needed to know, but a desperate sense of time slipping away was practically choking me.

"Listen, Professor Dreadful seems like a pretty bad guy. I don't know. He was nice enough to me. He opened my eyes to a lot of things..." (I did not say that he had been practically a second father to me. That is not a thing you say to your father.) "I don't really care about him right now. I owe my life, or at least my freedom and sanity, to my friends. It is ridiculous and unfair that these damned mermaids have them arrested. I don't care what their reason is. But most of all, I owe the most to this little girl named Abby. I made her a promise, a solemn promise. We are blood-brothers. I adopted her. Understand? She takes her orders from some gypsy called the Big Man. His name is Ron Barry."

"*Rombaro* is the Romani word for a chieftain or prince.

Strange. The gypsies are part of the Wisecraft. She should be in no danger from them."

"I did not say *she* was a gypsy. Abby was born an Urrasse. Her mother was a Christian, or at least a follower of John the Baptist. I don't remember the name of the aeon she is from. Abby is from a highly placed aristocratic family, but then her Mom was tortured to death. She was trained to be an assassin by a guy named Slaughterbench. He has a bunch of other names, and I swear I am going to kill him."

"Son, it is not wise to talk that way."

I nodded. I should just kill him without telling anyone beforehand. Good idea.

Aloud, I said, "My friend Knack is a Blemmyae, a monster race serving Ur. The mermaids probably have them both chained in a shark tank or something, thinking they are enemies. What I don't get is why they would arrest Foster. Unless… wait a minute… When Penny laid eyes on Foster, the first thing she did was dress him down. She was plenty mad. She called him a thief and burglar. And she's read *The Hobbit*, which I think is kind of cute."

His brow contracted. "Foster? Foster Hidden? He is a Wisecraft, too. He is Prussian, from an aeon called Riphath. I forget what the juncture event was. I think the miracle of Pope Leo turning back Attila the Hun never happened there."

And anger stirred in my blood. "You recognize the name? He is in my Scout troop. I hang out with him all the time. I've had him over to the house. You did not tell me? My best friend? His real name is Eflast Falinn."

"I am a man under discipline, my son. I have taken vows of obedience and silence. It was not my decision, but…" He sighed again and looked unhappy. "…I suppose I could have raised a bigger stink or even resigned my commission. But I just kept telling myself to relax because God had blessed me with a son who could not be hurt…"

"I can be hurt plenty!" I said. "When I am lied to. By everyone. My whole life. Then I find out. That hurts. But the hurt cannot kill me. So I cannot go to Heaven."

"Son, I promise you. So help me God. No more lies."

"What?"

"You are of age. You've survived a baptism of fire. The baptism of battle. You rescued Jonah of Arphaxad, who is the one man on whom all our hopes are pinned. So the Grandmaster can have no sound reason any more for shutting my mouth. Please forgive me. Is it a promise? I will have you officially knighted and in the Order, and you will be as much as part of this as I am. Join the family business. How does that sound?"

How did it sound? It sounded wonderful. I would be exactly what I always wanted to be, and the barrier between me and my Dad would be gone. The feeling of being outside, a feeling that had haunted me my whole life, would be gone.

I almost forgot to be angry. But there was one last thing.

"I'll forgive you," I said, "If you mean it. But why did you not tell Alexei about Mom? Where she is?"

Father gave me a long, hard stare. "What will he do the moment he finds out?"

"Easy question. Go try to rescue her."

"The only pathway open goes directly through deep Uncreation. Not even the most accomplished Ostiary can survive. Bathyspheres and spaceships do not work there, not in the deepest part. Even the transition vessels of the enemy, their wayships, have limits. Nothing mortal can survive."

"Well, he would still have to go. There is only one way to make sure something is impossible. I mean, you raised us. You know."

"I know. The raising is not done. Until my son is man enough to stand and wait when he is told to stand and wait, he is not a man. He cannot be trusted with hard truths."

I felt as if I had stepped into a pit and fallen down and down. I said, "I should have trusted you, Father. I knew you had secret work of some sort. I mean, it is obvious from the way we live. A good son would have simply known, simply rested on the solid truth, that any secrets his Dad kept from him, it was better not for him to know."

He nodded.

I said, "But you could have at least told me Foster was a gypsy. That would not spill any secrets."

6. Gypsy Boy

I wish now that I had had a camera in my hand because the look of utter dumbfoundedness is one I have never seen on my Dad's narrow, hard-edged face before or since. Also, he just kind of made a gulping noise, "Wh–Wha–Wh–?"

It was a great moment.

I said, "You did not know what Foster really was?"

"They kill gypsies on his world."

"He's not from there. He faked up his ID. He told me he was a master forger and very sneaky."

A look of wonder lit up Dad's eyes, and he snapped his fingers the way I do when I really like a thought I've had. Then, he threw back his head and laughed.

I said, "What is it? No more lies. Remember?"

He said, "No more lies, but you have to give me an oath of obedience, just as I gave the master who knighted me. I cannot tell you things that might endanger missions and men's lives without that oath."

I asked him for a Bible to swear on. He touched a small statuette, and it came to life, a little puppet. It was a telephone of some sort. He curtly asked the voice that answered to bring a Bible to "the Ante-Segnatura chamber in officer's country," which was evidently the name of the cabin I was in.

After the statuette closed its eyes again and Dad turned back toward me, I said, "What can you tell me that is not secret?"

"I can tell you why Penny hates Foster and called him a thief. Assuming your information that he is a gypsy..."

"I heard it from his own mouth."

"If that means anything. The Romani were the founders of the Wisecraft before their home world was taken. Leadership fell into other hands, and these other worlds pursued ever darker knowledge that the Romani lore would not have allowed. The Romani seek alliance with anyone willing to oppose the Dark Tower, including us; but the witches mistrust the Ecclesia. A rebel faction within the Wisecraft, called the *Patrin Pral*, the Brotherhood of the Leaf-marked Way, still follows the Romani philosophy."

"Foster is one? A *Pral*?"

"So I assume. A small, well-trained group broke the close at the mouth of the Rhine, where the main Circassian stronghold in Riphath is seated, and stole a great treasure or relic. I also know that the Circassians secretly established an undersea twilight-path leading to our world, which breaks more than one treaty they have with us. The relic, if it is what I suspect, is what allowed Foster to find and follow the secret undersea-path. It is how he smuggled himself into our world. I bet."

But I said, "No."

He looked surprised again. "No? Why not?"

"Because there is a simpler explanation," I said. "Mom told him how to get into our world. She saw the secret path from afar and told him where it was. I bet."

His look this time was beyond astonishment.

I was surprised at his surprise. He knew that Mom was trapped in the gypsy homeland of Sabtechah in the buried city of Agarththa. His letter had told me that.

I said, "The Dark Tower wants me because I can go there. I assume not even they can pass whatever block they set up. Their chief evil magician, Enmeduranki, told me I was going to destroy and defile the Seven-Ringed Grail of Jamshyd, which is in a place called the Psycho-something."

"Psychomanteum…" He muttered. "It is a divining chamber."

"You told me my whole life Mom is still watching us. She is watching them, too. With the Grail. Seeing what they do and how they do it." I frowned. "I may be confusing what the Dark Lord told me with what the Dark Lord's plumber told me. They are also invading a place called Raamah, where Kai Khosrow sleeps in Shazand. I remember that name because it is the same as what Billy Batson or Gomer Pyle says."

He barked, "Tell me how she got word out! Who talked to her? Is she well?"

I said, "Mother talked to a strega named Maleqorobar, who sent the message through a being called an Apsara, a spirit being or light elf that Foster's people worship and obey. Mom asked Foster to keep an eye on me. Foster also asked me officially and formally for fellowship and alliance with the Templars."

Dad closed his eyes, and I swear he wiped them. I did not think his tear ducts actually worked. He heaved a sigh of relief. A sigh? It was a sob.

Then, his eyes snapped open, and he was all business again. "In whose name?"

"What?"

"Foster asked for an alliance. Was he speaking for all the Wisecraft, for the Nightriders of Riphath, or just for the Chovexani?"

"He did not say. But he is here, and the mermaids have him. You can ask him after we save him."

7. Stronger than Fetters

Dad scowled. "If the Circassians have him, nothing will save him. If he is a member of a rebel faction, a traitor to their high command, should he be saved?"

"They're evil. He's my friend. And he was doing a favor for Mom!"

"If a man breaks faith with bad masters, even in a good cause, he betrays his word."

At that moment, a bell rang out a low and solemn note.

Dad stood. "I have to go. The Convocation is adjourning."

I said, "No! What you have to do is save the people I came with!"

"The Circassians agreed to cooperate with us in seeing each of your underage 'wives' home again or to find new homes to those who have no place to return to. The Church has been shipping refugees safely from dying worlds to safer ones for hundreds of years and has hospitals, schools, orphanages, holy orders... all the institutions we invented, ready to aid them. Aiding the sojourner, the poor, the widow, the weak, is one thing the Church has always done best. Do not worry on their behalf."

"I—I am glad for the girls, sure, but that is not who I meant," I said, "I mean my best friend, my girlfriend, my blood-sister, and my... my friendly pet monster!" (Okay, there is no way a grown and married man like Nack is anyone's pet anything, but I did not know how else to explain it. "The guy who decided not to eat me" does not put across the right gut feeling either, does it?) Scowling, I added, "Why are Christians making deals with witches anyway?"

"Why did Churchill make a pact with Stalin?"

I scowled. "Mom always said that the Devil laughs when a man says the ends justifies the means."

"He also laughs when little boys refuse to grow up." He stepped to the door and paused. "Do I need to lock this?"

"Dad! I am saving my friends! I rescued them all from the Dark Tower. I can rescue them from this drowned city! Or from you!"

The bell rang again. Again, the muscles in his jaw twitched. He had to go, but he had to stay and speak his piece. "Did I tell you why I thought the Circassians would arrest Penny?"

I shook my head.

"She was helping Achitophel Dreadful. He was within a few minutes of destroying every living thing on our world, from whales to amoebas, snuffing out the stars, and melting land, sea, and sky back into unlight primal chaos. He meant to direct the path of destruction toward Ur, to collapse the two aeons together."

I wanted to say something. Something clever to make these horrible words have no weight. I made a groping noise with my mouth, but no words came. "Uh—but—um—"

"Girlfriend or not, son, that woman is involved in the most serious crime I have ever heard tell of. The worst crime I can even imagine. All the genocides and massacres and murders in all history combined would be like nothing compared to the annihilation of two worlds."

There was no time to say everything I had to say. I could have said that, even if grown men like Knack could fend for themselves, Abby was a little girl. Even if Foster or Penny in some twisted way deserved their fate, Abby did not.

And I could not stand the thought of the mermaids and their songs toying with the mind and soul of a fourteen-year-old. At that moment, I hated the fair-skinned, clear-voiced sirens of this drowned and sunless floating city just as much as I hated the insane, gray-bearded, rheumy-eyed astrologers in their Dark Tower.

I said, "I am not abandoning Abby! She is my little sister just as much as I am your son!"

He turned his back. "And if your effort breaks up the alliance and we lose the war? I can make inquiries. Do nothing rash. Break no laws here, and do not offend our hostesses. Because this is not a test you can take over. There will be no second chance for you... or for me."

Sudden fears clogged my throat. I remembered Alexei saying Dad was going to be killed because of what I had done. I did not know what that meant.

The bell rang a third time. He spoke without turning his head. "Are you a man? I am telling you to stand and wait. Have I your word, Ilyusha? Your sworn word?"

I said. "Yes."

He did not close the door behind him as he left the cabin.

10

THEY ALSO SERVE

1. Clothes Make the Man

J was in the mood to mope, but I was interrupted. An orderly came by to act as my valet and then a barber and a tailor. Locker, showers, bar of soap, and straight razor soon followed.

The barber was a squat, smelly guy with a squint. Every tooth in his mouth was gold, and he was rude. I amused myself by making my hair unexpectedly expand and contract while he tried to give me a shave and a haircut.

He must have cut off five or six pounds of hair. I could still feel it, however. When no one was looking, I had my severed hair climb snakelike out of the trashbin behind the barbering station and wind itself into a rope. I suppose the easiest way to recombine it would have been to eat it, but I did not want to do that when anyone was looking, so I had the rope drape itself around my shoulders under my cloak.

I was spruced up and given a nice new white tunic with a big red cross on it and then a white mantle with an even larger red cross on it. It seemed that whoever designed my

Dad's money belt and Kevlar jacket also made brighter and more comfy versions for formal dress occasions. There was a plastron or breastplate. There was a baldric to hang Dancing Maiden.

An armorer issued me a *wakizashi*, or side-sword, to go with it. I had to sign for it. The armorer, a gruff man with a German accent and a prosthetic arm made of animated black ceramic, was vexed that I did not have signet ring to put a seal on the corner of the page, as I should have had.

I asked him about the birthdate of the side-sword; he just gave me an odd look.

Dad had not been kidding. Apparently, I was going to be allowed to keep his stuff. I would be allowed to wear the uniform of a squire before officially joining. This seemed odd, but it might have been so I did not look shabby in the eyes of the locals.

The orderly marched me back to the Ante-Segnatura chamber in officer's country. "Please wait here. You will be summoned to the Convocation soon." With this remark, he saluted and left.

And he left the door still open.

2. Happy Ending

For a few minutes, I strutted back and forth, looking down at my splendid uniform and brilliant white breastplate, wishing there was a mirror in the cabin. I was literally a knight in shining armor. I laughed, and I practiced a few stances and sword forms just to see how it felt while wearing a plastron.

I saluted an imaginary foe and performed a cutting pattern called *daruma otoshi*, a diagonal downward strike to an opponent's arm in the split second as he begins his stroke and is open; then, four swift horizontal strokes across unprotected neck, chest, belly, loins. I returned to first position, controlling my breathing, without taking my eyes from my foe as he fell to his death. I shook his imaginary blood free of the blade, sheathed it again, and then bowed at his honorable death, where he uttered no word of fear.

This was a happy ending. I had succeeded in what was apparently a crucial rescue mission. The escaped slavegirls were in safe hands. Each was going to be sent to her own home or to find a new one.

I was back with my dad and older brother and promised a life just what I always wanted: to be out doing heroic things. Knight-errantry. Saving damsels in distress. Slaying dragons. The whole organization of the Knights Templar was aimed at that. Alexei had said it: *We fight monsters.*

What could be cooler? The heroic life I always wanted was open before me like a yellow brick road, wonders leading to more wondrous wonders, and great deeds leading to greater deeds.

I straightened from the bow and saw the open door.

If this was a happy ending, why was I do darned unhappy?

Having killed real foes, it seemed childish to pretend to kill imaginary ones—even honorable foes. I could not see him any longer. I saw Abby's eyes, her big brown eyes, staring at me with hope and wonder.

I had promised her a happy ending also. Now she was in a jail, or in a fishtank, or mesmerized by siren singing, and I sat here and did nothing. I did nothing because of politics. Because an alliance with witches practicing black magic was what my father's superiors thought was prudent.

And what about Foster? What about Knack? Did I save Knack from one jail cell only to bring him to another?

And what about Penny, my beautiful Penelope?

A mad murderess. A mass-murdering witch.

And she was not mine. Why did I still want her to be? If my passion was just shallow mooning, just puppy love, just based on looks, I should cast it aside. So why didn't I? Why couldn't I?

I still believed in her. Somehow. But why?

I drew the scabbard so that I could sit down in the cabin's one chair. I glared at the open doorframe, mocking me. Like a rat running circles in a maze and never finding any exit, my thoughts scampered up and down the same twisted pathways.

I had also given my word to the Professor, long ago, to save his daughter. It had been a lie. He was not a professor, and she was not his daughter, and there had been no danger from which to save her. Did that excuse the oath? Because, no matter who she was, she was in danger now.

My promise to get Abby and the others home was also not excused.

I raised my eyes. The door was right before me, hanging open, unlocked, unclosed. It was inviting me. It beckoned.

Walking through it would break my oath to my father. Staying here and doing nothing would break my oath to everyone else.

My eyes were magnetized by the alluring open door. Only two paths lay before me. Both were dishonorable.

But would a hero, a real hero, be so concerned with his own honor? Would he be so worried about himself and his word? Or would he think first of those who needed him?

Maybe I was not suited to be a hero. Maybe seeking glory was folly.

But my friends needed me.

3. A New Thought

I leaned back and stared up at the overhead. I knew no

clear way to satisfy my duties to father and to friends. He might forgive me if I failed him. Them, if they were under arrest, might not have much time if I failed them.

A new thought occurred to me. I had not seen them get arrested. Or had I?

Just then, a sergeant in a black cloak came and saw me, sitting without motion, my eyes turned to Heaven. He probably assumed I was deep in prayer or something because he put a Bible gently on the writing desk, bowed toward it, and stepped backward to the door.

I said in Latin, "Begging your pardon, Sergeant, but when I came here. I was with friends, but I don't know what happened to them. By any chance, did anyone here in this embassy have the main gate leading into the outer sea under observation? Do you keep any records of the comings and goings here?"

He looked at me oddly. I wondered how bad my grammar was.

I said, more loudly and slowly, "I do not remember what happened after I came in. Came in the gate. The mermaids enchanted me. Singing magic. You understand? *La-la-la.* Malediction. It robbed my thought. I have no way to break the spell. But if our spies saw me enter, they saw all. Spies, are they here? Spies, here? Did they see? Do you know?"

He smiled crookedly and answered in heavily accented English. "Young squire, by the faith! Here you be, shiny as a new penny, green as a fresh shoot o' springtide, not even a proper recruit yet, and wrapping your tongue-wags up to what's as high over your head as a proud hawk at noon! Bend your ear up close to me: I will give you the right word, true as the King's coin. All these fabulous creatures and sights to make you sigh? Aye, and your mouth all open wide, enough to swallow flies as a frog, no doubt, and eyes as big as dinner plates. All these wise-women and their woven runes and chanted spells? We have something better on our world!"

"You are from Albion?"

"Better than Albion. I am from Scaefa!" He pointed dramatically at the Bible. "Here is the Word as spoke by the Ancient of Days, the High King of Highest Kings Most High, and the Lord of the Hosts of Heaven! Written in the blood of martyrs, every letter, every jot and tittle! Have you been shrived? Then fret no fretting! Set your heart on high things, and think no more on your poor self, burn bright your soul with prayer and fasting, fan the flame, and the curses of the crooked women will have no more power to confuse, confound, and befuddle or bedevil." He picked up the Bible and threw it in my lap. "Fear not. Fear nothing save the Lord, foolish boy."

A voice from somewhere down the corridor called the man away.

I closed my eyes, went to my knees, and said a prayer to saints Dymphna and Cyprian, the patrons of protection from madness and magic. And as I sat, I cleared my mind, controlled my breathing, and centered my thoughts.

Memory floated to the surface.

4. Repressed Memory

Once again, I was surrounded by a bubble that closed around us as we swam into the city. Once again, I saw the bubble sinking down and down toward a larger, darker bubble, one that seemed filled with ink, not water. Once again, beautiful girls swam and sported around me, alluring, laughing, teasing, and flirting, and one kissed me. Another handed me a cup of brine. It scalded my throat as I drank, and I had no time to spit it out. Coldness spread from mouth to throat to heart. Numbness flowed from sinuous, sensuous songs and passed over me, entering my ears and brain, bringing soothing darkness.

I groaned and pried my eyes open again. I was lying on a flat surface under a dark dome. Everything seemed weightless even though my nose told me I was in air, not water. The golden flail I had just been carrying was in a circle on the floor nearby. Singing sea-women were drawing out Urad-Betti from the glowing black ball of the nowhither space. A servant with a tray offered her a silver cup. When Urad-Betti drank it, her eyes went dull, her smile went blank, and she sank to the floor. Two sea maidens carried her to a place on the mats at the end of the line of sleeping girls.

Our one hundred and fifty girls were lying in thirty rows of five each, evenly spaced, draped in postures of slumber. Urad-Betti was the last one out of the black sphere.

Most of the slumberers were talking in their sleep, and beautiful sea maidens were hovering close, faces bent down to hear their words. The sea maidens would call softly to one another and move methodically from girl to girl. It was pretty clear that the sea maidens were trying to guess which unknown language was spoken by which sleeper, so a translator familiar with the tongue could be called over to listen.

Knack was here also. He was not yet asleep. His huge body was slumped over, shaking his shoulders in a woozy fashion. But his waist was split by a big, silly, sleepy grin, and the eyes in his chest were blank.

Penny was standing upright, her face stiff and expressionless with fear. Two of her sisters were holding her arms twisted up behind her back. A third sister, smiling coldly, held a coiling jade-green sea-snake near her neck like a cutthroat flourishing a menacing dagger.

All the shadows in this dark place pointed directly away from me. I was the source of light.

The crucifix at my neck was glowing with a soft, strange,

pure radiance. The cross was weightless, floating upward, tethered to my throat by its necklace of rosary beads.

Just at the edge of sight, where the shadows were thickest, I could see Foster on his hands and knees, looking dazed, and a little girl in a grinning monkey mask tugging fretfully at his arm, trying to help him up.

Of Ossifrage, I saw no sign.

A floating woman I now knew was Psamathe swam gracefully toward Foster, a cup of brine in her slender hand. She was frowning at Abby as if she had not expected to see her there. Psamathe stopped in midmotion and turned her eyes toward me, then Knack, and then the rows of sleeping girls, making a small gesture with her forefinger. Counting. She was counting the number of people here. Then, she looked over to where a serving girls held trays of cups, no doubt brought for us.

A woman spoke in my ear. I knew her, too. She was the brunette translator I was later to see in the throne room. She spoke in Latin, "Answer, O Hero, answer me true. What is your name? Whence come you?"

Thunder, not words, came out of my mouth, and the sound of rushing waters. Somehow the sound, louder than a trumpet blast, carried a clear sense, as if someone were speaking directly into the heart and soul.

"Demetrius of Sermium am I, Duke of Thessaly, and manservant of the Most High. Gladly, I embraced the spearheads of the persecutors rather than deny. I hail from the bright lands and paradise where grows the Tree of Life, sent by Philomena. I cast you forth from this boy's soul in the name and power of Christ. Begone!"

The brunette screamed like a steam whistle and threw herself backward. Or perhaps she was shoved. Psamathe and the dozen other women there stared in horror.

Unnoticed behind Psamathe, little Abby put her mask's

lips to Foster's ear. He raised his hand to his mouth, bit that fleshy part between the thumb and the forefinger hard enough to draw blood. (It is called the purlicue, in case anyone asks you). His sleepy eyes jerked open, and his body stiffened, but he made no sound. He looked around wildly and saw a dozen weightless, gorgeous witches cowering from me and not looking at him. He took a little object—it was a glass arrowhead—out from the lanyard around his neck. Funny. I recognized that lanyard. I was there at camp when he made it.

White mist came out of the arrowhead. Nothingness, a region where eyesight no longer worked, spread out from him like a parasol being opened. He wrapped himself and Abby in it. If they made any noise as they sneaked away, I did not hear it.

Because the women were singing at me again. Oddly, even though I did not understand the words, I could see little images and pictures in my imagination. Daydreams about Penny, about her lovely face and voluptuous curves. Lust. Another image of myself talking to my father. Lying to him. Another image of Vorvolac being thrown over the railing to his non-death. Breaking my oath.

They sang about everything I had done wrong. I could see little images of my past misdeeds dancing before me.

Their seductive voices drew me, and I stopped hearing the stronger, trumpet-roaring chords from Saint Demetrius. Sleep closed my eyes. Nothingness filled my brain.

5. If Seeing is Believing

I rose to my feet and crossed myself. Something the mermaids had stolen from my memory, I had found again.

I thanked and blessed whatever suspicious nature had

made me so reluctant to ask Psamathe about Foster or Abby by name.

Abby and Foster were alive and on the run, somewhere amid the canals and air-tubes and floating domes of Anthemoessa, the siren city: a boy who could not be seen and a girl who could not be predicted. Knack and Penny had fallen into the lovely, hostile hands of the sea-maidens. Ossifrage, I assumed, was safe since the mermaids felt free to tell the Templars I had saved him.

I looked at the door yet again.

My suspicious nature had served me well. It now whispered that rushing headlong into messes was precisely the thing unkillable abominations would always be tempted to do; it was precisely the thing a man who wanted, not applause, but only to save his friends, would not do.

So what to do? I know what a boy drunk with heroic dreams would have done: jumped headfirst out the door, eager for action.

But what would a man do? How could I find my way out of this tangle of oaths, obligations, friendships, and false friendships? How could I see which way to go?

I put my hand at my side and gripped the scabbard of Dancing Maiden. Her solid weight at my hip, the grace of the hidden steel, seemed to answer my question.

6. Then Unbelief is Blindness

Up until age twelve my instructor had been Master Kyuzo, a prune-faced wiry old man, who never smiled. After that, it was Master Shichiroji, round faced, stout, and bland, who never stopped smiling. Ironically, Shichiroji was the harder master than Kyuzo. He cared more.

But he imparted the lessons well.

In kendo it is called *ken* and *kan*, seeing with the eye and seeing with the heart. You never move your eyes from the eyes of the foe, nor do you look where you are aiming, lest he read your intentions. You use the side of your vision, the same way you behold the whole mountain while keeping your eyes pointed at the peak.

To strike is good; to counterstrike is better. When the foe launches his attack, he opens himself, and you have the opportunity to counterstrike before his stroke lands. Best of all was to launch the counterstrike preemptively, before the foe begins his strike, knowing his move before he makes it, using your heart to see. The motion of the blow must be large, strong, swift, and light.

All fencing is attack and defense, to strike and to wait. When waiting, the spirit must be striking with fury although the limbs are quiet; and when striking, the limbs are furious while the spirit waits.

The art was to watch and wait without thought, without anticipation, so that your enemy's motions are reflected in the mirror of your heart. The image of a flying arrow reflected in the glass is as swift as the arrow, but the mirror never moves. As the mirror face must be free of dust, so the heart must be free of fear.

For now, I would keep my eyes open, unblinking, but not looking where I aimed. Let me seem to be reading, sightseeing, joking, feasting. Let me seem to be doing anything other than seeking my friends, and I would surely find them.

Here in the drowned city on the drowned world, I was drifting in the dark. Literally. I had lost the sun. And Foster, he was invisible. Searching for him with the eyes in my head was no good.

My plan was to make no plans. The blow of the foe would fall. I would await it. I would be relaxed as a spring, which is motionless precisely when it is most tightly coiled.

I flipped open the Bible at random. It fell open at Corinthians.

For we walk by faith, not by sight.

A sign from the unseen world if ever I had seen one! And, lately, the unseen had been pretty reliable and the seen things not so much.

The first thing to do in my new plan was to do nothing and to trust in the Lord.

So I took off my breastplate and gear, stretched out on the hard cot, and napped.

AFTERWORD

**Next Volume of *A Tale of the Unwithering Realm*
—NOWHITHER: Captain No One —**

APPENDIX A: THE AEONS

This information comes from the Squire's handbook and field manual I read while in Anthemoessa. I add it here because you might find it useful. There are seventy-two known aeons. Each has a particular type of technology or magic, along with monstrous race (*prodigium*) native to each.

The Ecclesia rule nine aeons:

1. **Sasan:** This is the home of the City of Gold, which is the headquarters for the High Command. The art of bringing statues to life, and having them report events in far places, is native here. The first few years of the events of the Apocalypse have happened here. The aeon is overrun by the Urrasse, except for the Golden City and the Middle Eastern terrain she controls. There is active fighting here: a hot war.
2. **Scaefa:**The Celtic Church: A technological world, with vitalistic ray and gravitic ray technology,

radium rifles and wireless sights and finders, as well as air and space craft.

3. **Tiras**: The Russian Church: The *shamir* or Cutting Stone of Solomon was discovered in this aeon, from which various antigravity rays, death rays, disintegration rays, and madness-inducing rays are derived. The aeon is famed for its domed cities and the technology to revive corpses into motion.

4. **Tharsis:** The Spanish Church: The Therapeutae have destroyed all witches here. The medicine of longevity has been discovered. Airships & flying suits are in the air, and vast tunnel systems mind the ground. The art to train apes to reason and speak was developed. The Western Hemisphere is lost to the Urrasse.

5. **Brennus:** The Gallic Church: The technology here is based on galvanic alchemy, and includes animal magnetism, breathing gear, air craft and space craft. Overrun by Urrasse, except that French bases in Polynesia, Antarctica, and the Moon are holding out.

6. **Albion:** The Roman Church: A world of devastating weapons. Technology includes atomic, biological, chemical weapons, electronics, computers, air craft and space craft.

7. **Midas**, aka Togarmah, Antioeci: The Austrian Church: A world of alchemy based arts: Golems, Longevity, Gold-making, ornithopter automata, celestial levitation substances, sky cities.

8. **Amaterasu:** The Nagasaki Church: Smithcrafting arts can create weapons that slay werewolves. More miracles here than other aeons.

9. **Arce**: The Crusader Kingdom: A recent (and the only) successful rebellion against Ur. The

investigation of the Spear of Longinus allowed them to discover the art of creating artificial men.

Scaefa and Sasan created the Ecclesia in the 7th Century. Tiras and Tharsis joined in the 12th. Albion, Brennus, Midas, Amaterasu, Arce joined in the 18th and 19th.

The Wisecraft rule nine aeons:

1. **Thalassa**: Home of the Sirens or Sea-witches. First capital of the Wise, from whom they take their name. Himalayan islands are under Urrasse control. However, the Rocky Islands and Andes Islands are called the Island of the Wise, seat of the long-lived Cyrni, half-mermaids and magicians, selkie and sealmen. Thalassa is the old capitol of the Wisecraft. The sea-maidens can open the many large patches of twilight found below the sea. The forces are too widely separated to engage. No current fighting.

2. **Varvan**: Sorginak or Shadow-witches in service to the moon-goddess Mari. Ys, the witch-city, is a most ancient ally of Thalassa, but it was rendered desolate by a sub-sea volcano arising during the martyrdom of Saint Aymeric, who entered the forbidden capitol in the Twelfth Century to preach the gospel. The wise blame the Ecclesia for the disaster.

3. **Sabtechah:** Chovexani or clairvoyants. It is the Romani (gypsy) homeworld, and is entirely besieged. Central Asia obliterated. A besieging force only, no current fighting.

4. **Cush**: Strega or Dream-witches. The current capital of the Wise, where refuges from Riphath

have fled. Cush is overgrown with jungles created by centuries of pulling seeds from the dreamlands into the material realm, and the unwillingness of the worshippers of the small gods to desecrate 'high places'. The Strega know the art of Eosphormancy, the driving back of twilight by means of archangel light made visible.

5. **Svan**: Zduhac or Storm-Witches. The war here is stalemated, as the storm witches have flooded lands from the Island of Spain to the Sea of Ob, so that the European Archipelago is cut off from Urrasse troops in Africa. The Urrasse horoscopes tell them merely to wait for a century, as the Zduhac have offended their totemic spirits by the abuse of their power to raise up, rather than allay, storms. Raiding and small actions only.

6. **Amorreus**: Artabtatitae, also called Witches of the Wild, or theriomancers. Speech with animals is practiced here. The wise here have familiars called fetches, who can call forth and solidify beast-spirits or blood-shadows representing a man's soul or his fate.

7. **Dagon**: Sedeclahot or Ghost-witches. Daughters of Sedecla practice necromantic divination, and thus can anticipate, and at times elude, Urrasse astrologers.

8. **Riphath**: Svartalfwissen or Darkelves. Tarncraft allows the warlock to assume a shadow like a cloak, which he can mold to any shape of beast or man; to cast his shadow to distant lands and seem to stand in two places at once; to enter the twilight and pass through to other aeons. Conquered throughout Asia and Africa, and only Europe is still under control of the Nachtritter. The New

World is undiscovered, albeit Ur has plans to conquer the Aztec empire there in due time. The Black Forest in Germany, for reasons not clear, is the source of frequent, large, and dense manifestations of Twilight. There is hot fighting here.

9. **Uenuku:** Tohunga Makutu. The medicine men here practice skin-changing, and can become dolphins or ride whales. In distant continents can be found swan maidens and living rainbows.

Rhodanim is an aeon contacted by Riphath, claimed by the Wise, but this claim is disputed by the Ecclesia. Its seas have turned to blood, and many refugees seek escape to other worlds.

The Urrasse rule 33 Aeons.

1. Panchaea
2. Mizraim
3. Elam
4. Asshur
5. Phut
6. Nuwa
7. Heth
8. Evilas
9. Abtuat
10. Sheba
11. Sidon
12. U-Tixo
13. Thoebel
14. Gath
15. Manu
16. Arvad
17. Ud

18. Taari
19. Javan
20. Chittim
21. Viracocha
22. Enoch
23. Cainem
24. Thalassa
25. Sotuknang
26. Pethor
27. Noy
28. Ashkinaz
29. Mosoch
30. Astabor
31. Arphaxad
32. Uz
33. Ul

The count of aeons ruled by Urrasse would be higher, if it included **Vasumati, Pha, Cimer,** or included **Ur** itself.

Vasumati was the source of the sole resistance to the Dark Tower, in ages before the Wisecraft arose, it was obliterated utterly.

Pha was likewise obliterated because the Soul-Extracting Lamas inquired too deeply into astrology, and had an art to rival the Darkest Tower.

Cimer has troops stationed in it, but the scattered neolithic tribesmen of the world have no towns nor cities to conquer, no trade, nor crops, and the peoples make poor slaves. It was not considered a conquest because no pitched battles have ever been fought here, merely police actions to drive off raiding parties.

Unaligned Aeons

Certain aeons are known to exist, but have neither been invaded by the Urrasse, beguiled by the Wisecraft, or been sent missionaries by the Ecclesia.

Selah, called **Arphaxad**

This is a case where a parent aeon branched, and the natives make contact with the Wise, through mutual friends among the gypsies, before the Urrasse was aware of the new world.

Aragaladi

The Great Flood came and slew all those on Earth, and their bones became rocks. Certain o the wise were preserved in the Long-Ago Dreamtime, and when they emerged again, all was oceans and rocks. The shades of the dead called on heaven. Their bones grew large and became dry land, and their tears made the soil fertile again. The Wise of Aragaladi can walk through dreams, and see what men see in their sleep.

Raamah

This is an aeon where Nimrod's brother overcame him, and the men of the Erythraean Island learned the art of baiting twilight, and closing the Moebius gates. The world is one that cannot be reached unless those living there should halt their arts.

Yu

The dragons of this aeon have taught to men the art of geomancy, which allows them to manipulate the Earth Current in such a way as to prevent the formation of twilight sufficient to open a gate. In effect, the Imperial Capital has ordered all other worlds blocked off.

APPENDIX B: THE MONSTROUS RACES

Each aeon has a particular monstrous race (*prodigium*) native to it. Listed below by name, native aeon, and loyalty.

Abarimones
Backward-footed men from the Himalayas capable of running at great speeds.
Native to Gath (an aeon conquered by Ur).

Aigipanes
Goat-legged and horned men who lived in the Atlas Mountains of Libya.
Chittim (Ur)

Androleteirae (also called **Amazons**)
Warrior women. Here, originally the daughters of Mars, settled in Gallic lands. From their line sprang both Bradamante and Marfisa, who saved Charlemagne from the Saracen, preserving the Church.
Brennus, See of the Gallic Church in (Ecclesia)
This race is also found in Madai.

Androphagi
Cannibals who live entirely on the flesh of men.
Abtuat (Ur) – The Blemmyae are also native to this aeon, and
have adopted this horrid practice.

Arimaspians (also called **Monommatoi**)
One-eyed Scythian men who war with the griffins in the
Riphaean Mountains for gold.
Taari (Ur).

Artabatitae
A tribe of African men who travel around on all fours like
apes, and learn the speech of birds and beasts.
Amorreus (Wisecraft).

Astomi
A hair-covered and mouthless tribe who live solely off the
scent of aromatic plants.
Ud (Ur).

Autochthons (also called Those Who Seek for Death in
Vain).
Immortals who ate from the Tree of Life.
Cainem (Ur).

Blemmyae (also called Sternophthalmoi)
A tribe of headless men whose faces are set upon their chests
Abtuat (Ur) – The Androphagi are also native to this aeon.

Calingi
Short-lived men, matured at five and gray-haired by eight,
derived from the Spartoi grown of dragons' teeth by
Cadmus. Given souls and long lives by crusader magic.
Arachis in the See of the Jerusalem church (Ecclesia).

Catoudaei
Troglodytes of a subterranean race commanding a primordial energy called Vril-ya
Ashkinaz (Ur).

Choromandae
A tribe of men with hair-covered bodies, dog's teeth and a horrible scream in place of speech.
Sheba (Ur).

Cimmerians
A race immune to ghosts.
Cimer. (Ur). – Also native to this aeon are the Hippopodes.

Cruorbibitors (also **Bloodquaffers**).
Vampires created by alchemy by the descendants of Alexander the Great.
Found in Javan and Elishah (Ur).

Cynocephali (also **Lycanthropes**)
A tribe of invulnerable wolf-monsters from Romania.
Evander, called Thoebel (Ur).

Cyrni
A tribe of long-lived men who are never touched by signs of old age. Antediluvians.
These are found in the aeons of **Enoch, Shinar, Thalassa**. It is a matter of debate to which aeon they are native. Enoch and Shinar are controlled by Ur. Thalassa is beholden to the Wisecraft.

Daeva
A race of ascetics who developed infinitely powerful weapons called *astra*.

Vasumati (Obliterated by Ur)

Dragons (also, **Long**)
A race of serpentine spirit-beings who possess glorified bodies.
Yu. (Unaligned)

Gaeagenes
A tribe of six-armed, earth-born men fought by the Argonauts on Bear Mountain in Mysia.
Ul (Ur).

Gaetuli
A nation in north Africa, whose dervishes who sleep in the tombs of the dead to learn the shadows of the future. Evilas (Ur) – Also in this aeon is found the Panotii.

Gorgades
Inhabitants of the island of the Gorgones in the Arctic. The women have hair all over their bodies, and the men were so swift of foot that they can outrun stallions.
Noj (Ur).

Gypsies (also **Romani**)
Have the second sight.
Sabtechah (Wisecraft).

Heliades
Inhabitants of seven happy islands in the Southern Ocean. Hairless, with bendable bones, and a double-tongue which allows them to hold two conversations at once.
Astabor (Ur).

Hemicynes

Men possessed by wolf spirits, also blessed with the ability to withstand certain vibration levels of the ether dangerous to other people.
Tiras in the See of the Russian Church (Ecclesia).

Hippopodes
A race of horse-hoofed bipedal men.
Cimer. (Ur). – The Cimmerians are also native to this aeon.

Homunculi
Artificial persons and golems including natural persons artificially elongated, also called Struldbrugs.
Midas, the See of the Austrian Church (Ecclesia).

Illyrii
The witches of Illyria, whose prayers cause meadows to dry up, trees to wither and infants to perish; who also bewitch with a glance and who kill those they stare at for a longer time, especially with a look of anger, and that their evil eye is most felt by adults; and that what is more remarkable is that they have two pupils in each eye. Mosoch (Ur).

Lares called Leprechauns
Spirits made of subtle matter than can materialize via an ectoplasm. Gremlins are a type of bred Lares.
Scaefa, in the See of the Celtic Church (Ecclesia).

Locusts
Chimera of the apocalypse infesting the golden city.
Sasan, in the See of the Assyrian Church. (Ecclesia)

Machlyes
A Libyan tribe of androgens.
Phut (Ur).

Macrocephali
Men with oversized heads, blessed with deep and agile intelligence.
Asshur (Ur).

Marsi
Said to be descended from the son of Circe. Immune to snakes.
Manu (Ur) — This aeon contains also Pygmaioi.

Melanochroti
A tribe of black-skinned men ruled by a king with a single eye in the middle of his forehead. (here the skin iron-hard) Arvad. (Ur).

Nahayeye
Artificial men created out of mud, sticks, or flowers.
Sotuknang (Ur).

Nyctalopes
Night-seeing men from Albania. Gray eyed. Born bald.
Lud (Ur).

Oeonae
The name means 'egg eaters'. A race of Nephilim who impregnate demons into their unborn.
Enoch. (Ur).

Ophiogenes
A race of Trojans descended from a dragon. It was said that a mere touch from one of these people could cure snakebite. This was due to the fact that a progenitor of the race had changed from a snake to a human being.
Uz (Ur).

Panchaeans.
Atheists living in the great island of Panchaea in the Arabian sea, in the utopian city of Panara. Golden pillars there record that the gods are merely kings flattered with absurd exaggerations.
Sheba called Panchaea (Ur).

Panotii
A fabulous northern European tribe with gigantic, body-length ears.
Evilas (Ur) — Also in this aeon are found Gaetuli.

Patagonians.
Giants able to withstand extreme cold.
Aragaladi (unaligned)

Phalachroi
A sacred Scythian tribe, blessed like their neighbors the Hyperboreans. Can sleep for six months at a time. Men and women are both bald since birth. They never carry weapons, dwell in forests and live on berries. Their manners are mild, and all their neighbors refer disputes to them. Deemed a sacred race, all are careful not to molest nor moil with them. They are protected by an unseen and invincible power that renders bearing visible arms obsolete.
Elam (Ur).

Pharnaces
Men whose sweat and spittle is deadly venom
Viracocha (Ur).

Pterophoroi also called **Cloudwalkers** or **aal-Shem**.

They have the power of levitation and can walk into heaven and speak with the blessing dwelling there.

These hail from the aeons of Selah, but are wrongfully thought to come from Arphaxad (Disputed)

Pygmaioi (also called **Pygmies**)

Miniature men who war on cranes.

Manu (Ur) — This aeon contains also the Marsi.

Roswellians (also called **Grays**)

So called from the first known landing site. Aery creatures that look like bald gray-skinned large-eyed, midgets. Wrongly thought to issue from Mars or another planet is space.

Albion, See of the Roman Church (Ecclesia).

Sauromatae

Sons of Amazons and Scythians, able to fast indefinitely. Can neither die of starvation nor thirst. Among them, no virgin is permitted to marry until she kills a foe in the field.

Madai. (Ur)

Sciapods

A tribe of one-legged, one-footed Libyan men. The sciapod shelters himself from the sun beneath a giant, upraised foot. For this reason they were known as umbrella-foot or shadow-foots.

Utixo (Ur)

Sciritae

A tribe with snake-like nostrils in place of the nose, and bandy serpentine legs.

Nuwa (Ur)

Sedeclahot
Witches who speak to ghosts
Dagon (Wisecraft).

Shikigami
Familiar spirits summoned by a Taoist astrologers or
onmyoji.
Amaterasu in the See of the Nagasaki Church (Ecclesia).

Sirens also called **Sea-Witches**, **Sea-Maidens** and **Maleficae
Maris**
Amphibious witches whose songs command the sea, and
beguile men.
Thalassa (Wisecraft).

Soractes
Able to walk through fire unharmed or eat hot coals. From
Tibet.
Pha (Obliterated by Ur)

Sorginak
Witches able to bind and release imps, nymphs and giants.
Varvan (Wisecraft).

Strega
Witches able to summon, bind, release, and walk into
dreams.
Cush (Wisecraft).

Struthopodes
The men have feet one cubit long but the feet of the women
are so small that they are called Sparrow-feet
Heth (Ur)

Svartalfwicken
Warlocks taught the arts of summoning elfish mist, twilight, doppelgangers and the arts of invisibility.
Riphath (Wisecraft).

Syrbotae
A tribe of twelve-foot tall African men.
Sidon (Ur)

Theraputae
Essenes able to forgive sins, banish witchcraft.
Tharsis, See of the Spanish Church (Ecclesia).

Tohunga-Makutu
Shamans and skin-changers who speak to the sea monsters
Uenuku (Wisecraft).

Urrasse
The single primal and panhuman race that pre-existed all deviations into branches.
Shinar (Ur)

Zduhac
The witches who wrestle the wind, call or ally storms.
Svan (Wisecraft).

ABOUT THE AUTHOR

John Wright is a retired attorney and newspaperman who currently works as a technical writer. This spring, he was nominated for five Hugos. He lives in fairy-tale-like happiness with his wife, the authoress L. Jagi Lamplighter, and their four children, Orville, Ping-Ping, Roland and Just Wright.

He blogs at: http://www.scifiwright.com/

Superversive Press is a small press that specializes in heroic and uplifting fiction. To find out more visit out website

http://superversivepress.com

Also check out our Superversive News site

http://superversivesf.com

Don't forget to sign up for our mailing list while you're there

If you enjoyed this book please leave a review

Made in the USA
Middletown, DE
27 July 2019